The Bluebell Bunting Society

Poppy Dolan lives in Berkshire with her husband, where she is a keen baker and crafter as well as a prolific author of many laugh-out-loud romantic comedies, including the bestselling *The Bad Boyfriends Bootcamp*.

You can get in touch with Poppy on Twitter @poppydwriter and on Facebook at PoppyDolan-Books. She doesn't bite. Unless you are a dark chocolate digestive.

Also by Poppy Dolan

POPPY DOLAN

The Bluebell Bunting Society

CANELO

First published in the United Kingdom in 2017 by Canelo

This edition published in the United Kingdom in 2022 by

Canelo
Unit 9, 5th Floor
Cargo Works, 1–2 Hatfields
London, SE1 9PG
United Kingdom

A CIP catalogue record for this book is available from the British Library.

Print ISBN 978 1 80032 807 5
Ebook ISBN 978 1 91159 125 2

Look for more great books at www.canelo.co

Printed and bound in Great Britain by Clays Ltd, Elcograf S.p.A.

1

For Kirsty Greenwood. Man, oh man, I owe you so much.
Thank you for every single thing you've done for me.

Chapter 1

'If you're happy and you know it, clap your hands!'

But Alfred is not happy. Alfred is a furious ball of baby fat, a small and rather angry Winston Churchill lookalike. Tears are streaming down his red face and his screams are so forceful I can feel my fringe being blown off my forehead.

His screeches completely drown out my claps, but I persevere with the next verse. I thought singing soothed babies? I'm no Mariah, but even my off-key warbling shouldn't cause this kind of a reaction.

'...Stamp your feet!'

Alfred's mum looks like she could stamp on my head. I hear, as the world's angriest baby pauses to take a breath, 'It's not like this at Bounce and Rhyme.' The fellow uber-mum next to her, in identical skinny white jeans, nods with a sour frown, wrinkling her perfectly blended eyeshadow into crow's feet. Oh cripes. These two were the only new visitors this week, as well.

I

The whole idea of the Sunday Funday at the Hall was to give families a breather, a bit of a laugh, with craft activities and singing and general mucking about; kids everywhere and parents able to sip at weak squash and discuss extension plans. Well, that's what it had been like when I was little. Now I'd be happy to see a horde of happy mums and their buggies through the doors, whatever they wanted to do. Kickboxing. Astral meditation. Amateur acupuncture. But somehow I doubt Alfred's mum will be giving us a big grin emoji on Mumsnet and promoting our community space. I should have known she was a tough customer when her tot came dressed in tweed trousers, a cashmere roll neck and answering specifically to Alfred. This kid was no Alfie. Never *ever* an Alf. This toddler has better shoes than me. And I'm 29.

OK, so the damp patch above the fireplace and the crack running down next to the front door aren't exactly welcoming to most newcomers. And it gets a bit chilly when not full of bodies. And I didn't think to bring in anything other than bog-standard tea and coffee, and some lemon Robinsons.

'No decaf? No sugar-free?' White Jeans number 2 said in alarm, as if I'd suggested she give her little Tallulah a Haribo salad for lunch.

But the Hall has its charms, and I love it. I'm proud to be its caretaker, for want of a better title. I love its ornate ceiling roses, the mostly-intact tiles that form a beautiful scene at the doorstep – vibrant bluebells against a lush green hill. It might smell of mould. It might only have two, temperamental plug sockets. But William Hibbert left it to our village as a gift spanning the generations: he built it so we'd have a place to gather. A place to be. A real community hall. The problem is, the community seem to have forgotten. He built it in 1866, so I can't blame them.

Whether they've forgotten or they don't like the odd bit of peeling plaster flaking onto their heads, it's up to me to make Bluebell Hall as inviting as a freshly-made bed with extra kittens.

Because Bluebell Hall needs visitors. And fast.

I half-heartedly wave off my pair of yummy mummies: they won't be back.

There's a polite nudge in my side. 'You can't win them all,' Susannah says kindly. Even when I have a zero turnout for a Sunday, Susannah is always here with sympathy and Coffeemate. She was one of my Gran's best friends for decades, so just seeing her shiny silver bob and upright posture makes me feel calm, like I'm about to watch *Stars in Their Eyes* in my pjs in 1996, with a cheeky hot Nesquik on my Gran's sofa.

'Well, I appreciate you, caffeine,' I mutter, 'even if no one else does. Shall I make tea? Who else do we have left, should I make it a big pot?'

I scan the Hall. It's not big – not big enough for a wedding reception these days, more's the pity – but bigger than the Scout hut and definitely roomy enough for the smattering of locals we have today. There's Lucy and her boy, Abel, my unofficial godson. Lucy married my best mate from school, so I pretty much invited myself into the role and no one has disputed it since. I've also helped myself to the role of her best friend since she moved to Hazlehurst from London, and she's yet to make a formal complaint about that. Whoever said that women don't like the wives their male mates end up with clearly has not met this impressive lady. I think being her friend has improved my intelligence and maturity by at least 12 per cent. Bless Luce, she knows how desperate I am for bodies through the door, so she comes rain or shine, even when she's been working super hard and would rather flop about with a supplement and a Jammie Dodger on a Sunday. But here they are, sticking bits of sugar paper onto other bits of sugar paper, deep in serious four-year-old conversation. Every now and then, Abel will put his hands on top of Lucy's, to show her precisely where's she's going wrong and it makes my heart go all fluttery behind my ribs.

There are two of the Carter boys from down the street. A big, jolly family – if I could measure the Hall's attendance by volume alone, they would count for at least ten grown men. They are bouncing beach balls against the wall with huge slapping sounds, but seeing as I hardly have a pristine paint job to protect, I just let them get on with it. Their mum is lovely and I'm genuinely happy to take two of her five for an afternoon if it means her own house goes down to the mere 90 decibels.

Aha. Another new mum has slipped in and is looking with interest at our big carved panel memorialising William Hibbert, while her toddler picks up wooden blocks and lets them clatter to the floor with glee. Again, I do my best with the parquet but I'm not precious about it. People before parquet, is my motto. Here's another chance to butter up a potential regular. And the first step, as always in this great land of ours, is with a beverage.

'Hello! I'm making some drinks. Can I get you tea or coffee? I'm Connie, by the way.'

The mum turns on the spot, sending her swoop of bright red hair into her eyes. She quickly brushes it back then holds out her hand. 'I'm Flip. Philippa really but I was one of three Philippas at school so this

5

was the only shortening left. I would love a tea. Don't suppose you have Earl Grey?'

Ah. Another Former Londoner, I reckon. Still, she doesn't have white jeans on, so I mustn't lump her with the yummies just yet.

'I don't think so, sorry, but I will double check. Are you... new in town?'

'Yes! Moved here three weeks ago, from Walthamstow. I'm fascinated by the history.' She points up at the likeness of Hibbert on the wall, 'It's a bit unreal now to think of super rich people just dishing out money for the good of us commoners, isn't it?'

For a second I'm struck too dumb to reply. She's gone from London to full-blown Hazlehurst devotee in a few weeks. This is so promising.

When I don't quite get it together to reply, she talks on, gathering pace. 'But I shouldn't start down that road! No politics on a Sunday, so my other half always tells me. But I loved the village feel we had back in our old place and I really want to be part of it here too.' Flip suddenly grabs my wrist as she says this. If her neighbourly skills are as good as her grip, she has nothing to worry about. I shake my hand behind my back to regain some feeling.

'Well, we are very happy to have you here! The Sunday Funday is all about togetherness, and it's just one of many activities we run here to get the community sharing pastimes and good times.'

Flip's well-drawn eyebrows do a joyful wriggle. 'Oooh! Such as?'

'Um, well, the Bluebells meet here – it's sort of our local version of Girl Guides. We used to have a coffee morning but the old folks' home had to pull out because of...' My eyes roam to the baggy water marks on the ceiling and the storage heater on the wall so cantankerous it belongs in a home itself, 'health and safety red tape. Though it doesn't stop our old folks' choir coming, The OAP Three. They're a local institution, been singing together since the fifties and they say they'd rather break a hip than sing anywhere else. Plus, I think it's the only outing they get most weeks.'

Flip nods. 'What about the WI, does that meet here?'

Susannah trots past at a fast but still regal pace, chasing a deflating beach ball. 'Not since 1973, dear, when we had a fall out over sandwich spreads.'

'Shame. I'm dead keen on joining. And this would be such an atmospheric meeting space!'

I can tell Flip must do something creative, as she's really embracing our shabbiness as something more shabby chic, as if we've let the wallpaper peel on purpose and ripped out a brand-new bathroom suite to install legitimately chipped and faulty WCs from the Victorian period.

Abel runs over, proud to show me his own burst of creativity: lots of green and brown blobs of paper stuck on the inside of an old cereal box. My gran was forever collecting cereal boxes, egg boxes, wrapping paper – anything she deemed a 'resource' for the Hall. We may have been left the building itself but funds for what went on inside were a bit thin on the ground.

I'm cooing over its brilliance, all the while making a wide-eyed appeal to Luce for some help as to what it actually might be.

'He's got the triceratops' horns just right, don't you think?'

'Yes, yes,' I agree heartily. 'A right old Damien Hirst in the making.'

'Why's Damian thirsty?'

I think for a minute. 'Hirst. He's a modern artist who cuts cows in half and puts them in big jars.'

I should have thought for longer. Both Abel and Flip's daughter instantly start to wail.

–

When I come back from digging out emergency lolli-pops from the bottom of a Funday box of resources, Luce and Flip are chatting away, ten to the dozen. With the kids appeased and Abel leading little Sophie round the hall on a 'dino hunt', I tune back in to what they're saying.

'I'm not a local either, but I married one so I know all the Hazlehurst oddities now.'

'Hey!' I poke her in the ribs. 'We're not odd. We're just not, you know… cosmopolitan. We're old school.'

Lucy barks a laugh. 'You're so old school you might as well put the girls in mop caps and the boys in breeches!'

I fold my arms. 'Hardly. I tweet. I hashtag. I'm not yet in my third decade, old lady.'

'I'm ten months older than you.'

I press my lips together into an irritating smug smile. 'Old. Er.'

So Lucy goes looking for allies. 'This one,' her thumb jabs in my direction, 'might as well sleep with The Reader's Digest under her pillow at night, she is that stuck in the past. I suggested she run some adult only evening classes here, seeing as she's so keen to boost attendance. I did a knicker sewing class on a hen do once and it was so much fun.'

'I love sewing!' Flip claps and does a little jig. 'I would absolutely be up for something like that. And a blessed evening out of the house? Yes please, I'll come along twice if that's allowed.'

Lucy slings her arm round my neck to half-hug, half-strangle me. 'Sounds good, doesn't it? But Connie says what she always says when she's faced with something new.' She releases me with a sigh.

Well, if she's gathering troops, so am I. 'Susannah?' I yell across to our tiny kitchen. 'What would Gran say to sewing frilly undies in the Hall?'

Her neat face pops through the serving hatch. 'Hells bells, no!'

I shrug. Gran ran this place for 40 years and she knew just what the community needed and wanted. I'm not messing with that.

'Shame,' Flip says kindly. 'I'm working on having an entirely me-made wardrobe by 2020 and I'd forgotten all about underwear. So to speak!' She gives an enjoyably juicy cackle, with her hands clamped over her mouth.

Just then the Hall gets an unusual burst of activity: a balding middle-aged man shuffles in, followed by a teenage girl in very stompy boots. Abel gives a very loud pterodactyl shriek right in Sophie's face, which starts her screeching again; the Carter boys start rolling round the floor in a play fight, picking up sticky bits of sugar paper on their jumpers and using language I don't think their mum would be OK with. I try to prise them apart while simultaneously giving the two newbies in the doorway a welcoming grin. It might look a bit more like a grimace if I'm honest.

The teen's eyes, smudged in thick blue liner, narrow as they take in the childish chaos and my half-hearted attempts to dampen it. 'Lame!' she hisses, turning on her platform heel. Her dad (from his look of weary exhaustion, I can only assume he's the father) follows a safe ten paces behind, wincing at me in apology.

When everyone is calm and seated with a beaker of milk and a digestive, I finally exhale. Another missed opportunity for Hall-goers. More locals who'll see this place as a mouldering shed to be happily forgotten about.

Gran, I think, I miss you.

—

My noisy band of Funday-goers has dribbled away, and I'm now pushing a broom around as Susannah rinses teacups in the sink. Still, at least we do the tidying up together. Together. The word clatters around inside my head.

'No!' The broom clatters against the tiles as I make a dash for the log book. I've just realised that neither Flip nor the yummies signed in. Oh bums. Triple bums. A log book, one of those funny leather-bound things you see in fusty B&Bs, may be ridiculously old-fashioned but it holds the key to the Hall's future.

The Hall, such as it is – tiny, crumbling and obscure – is protected by the Hibbert estate for as long as half of the village population use it on a monthly basis. Hibbert's family line ended a few generations after he passed in the First World War, so his property and investments were taken over by a trust, and they were the ones to pay the caretaker and keep a casual eye on attendance levels. For more than 100 years it was easily achieved because the village was made up of about 200 people and most of them had a reason to spend time here: the Bluebells meetings, coffee mornings for the old folks, birthday parties for little ones, even a line-dancing class way back in the mists of 1993. But then ten years ago a brand spanking new housing estate was built just outside the village, sending the population numbers through the roof just as the roof of Bluebell Hall took a battering from a huge storm and covered the coffee morning and its blue-rinsed members in hail and splinters of oak.

Since then the new leisure centre on the estate has been crammed full of happy families on the weekends and Bluebell Hall has seen some pretty amazing dust bunnies. As locals splash in the pool or squeak about the squash court in their trainers, funnily enough they don't hanker after a draughty hall with scary loo facilities. (The spiders in there could be classified as small rodents, they are so big and hairy.) Hazlehurst village has never been such a vibrant place to be: new shops and restaurants have popped up to meet the big swell of inhabitants, the park got more funding and a new play area, even the library happily responded by stocking DVDs and magazines all of a sudden. But Bluebell Hall has just got lonelier and lonelier.

I shouldn't care, really. I'm not even 30, I'm unattached, I'm reasonably intelligent on a good day. I should be out making a kickass career for myself or falling in love and having twenty screaming Alfreds of my own. Or I should be taking in a Chilean sunset or developing an app. However it is apps are developed. I'm thinking it involves a calculator and lots of squared paper. Once upon a time, when turning 30 was just a vague threat on a far-away horizon, I had this mad idea of running music festivals (probably just a way I saw myself getting free gig tickets). That mad idea ended up going the way most mad ideas do – nowhere. Turns out, it wasn't the job for me. But caring about Bluebell Hall is not only my job now, it's in my bones. It's in my DNA.

When William Hibbert (Hibbs, as he's known in my family) bequeathed the Hall to the village, he also set up a bursary to pay a caretaker to look after it. And many great-greats ago, that was my ancestor Bob

Duncan. Since then, we Duncans have kept our eye on the Hall, barring great wars and the like proving a distraction. The last caretaker before me was my gran, Rosemarie. The first female caretaker here, but not the last. She walked in lilac slippers, did my gran, but she was no pushover. So when her own father suggested the mantle passed to her new husband, Reg, she promptly picked up his dinner plate and slid his Sunday roast with all the trimmings neatly out of the kitchen window. She told me, when I was a teenager, that she was very careful not to actually chip the plate as it was her mum's best, and she was no fool. And I took it as a really good lesson on how to stick up for yourself: don't be afraid to make a noise, but avoid permanent damage if you can.

Gran was such a passionate believer in the Hall and its place at the heart of our village. I flip back to the first page of the heavy log book: 1983. About ten years into Gran's long run as caretaker. She did hat decorating classes here, a homework club for after school, even ran her own keep fit. As I remember it, they just did lots of marching on the spot while a Rick Astley vinyl played on loop and Mrs Macomber from two roads over caught my gran up on the gossip. But that pretty much is the healthy heart of village life, to my mind.

Gran's only failing was that she was no Handy Andy. After my grandad died at the very unfair age of 65, she had no one to help with the maintenance of the building itself and the bursary didn't stretch to paying third parties. I think, too, that by that time my Gran was blind to the wonky or smelly bits of the Hall: she loved it. It was part of her fabric. It was probably why she wouldn't give up the caretaker's role, even in her eighties. And with fewer visitors, there were fewer pairs of eyes to notice. I was at university in Manchester while the Hall was starting to really fall apart. I was studying Philosophy, with a completely philosophical take on the rest of my life. In other words, I had no idea what I was going to do. I was really into bands back then. I was volunteering on the student newspaper, writing reviews of tiny bands in tiny pubs and I was too busy to come home much. I actually love all kinds of music – give me pop, reggae, soul, rock, even German new wave synth if the mood strikes, and I'm happy. But back then it was my big guitar band phase and that scene only really happened in late, loud, boozy places. So catching a 7.30 a.m. train down South for a family lunch slipped off my to do list. I feel a horrible cold clutch to my heart now that I didn't take more time to talk to Gran then, or listen to her updates on the Bluebells.

My fingers flip through the years, eighties and nineties and noughties. Until I reach Gran's last year in charge and her very last entry: the Bluebell camping trip. We have our own slightly odd version of the Girl Guides in Hazlehurst – the Bluebells. Again, thank good old Hibbs. He thought that the 'poor girls' of the village would benefit from lessons on deportment, manners and needlepoint, so his daughters formed this little club and they all pinned bluebells to their dresses and used the Hall as their headquarters. I think Hibbs had visions of it spreading all around the globe and turning out thousands of sweet, sewing misses but there was only ever one other faction, in Ontario, Canada: one of his daughters moved there when she married and started a new Bluebell gang, out of homesickness I shouldn't wonder.

Gran was the Bloom Mistress (pretty much a Brown Owl) as well as caretaker, and seeing as getting modern girls to embroider a psalm was a tall order, she started making up new activities for them – a camping trip (sleeping bags inside the Hall), lessons on everything from car maintenance to how to make the perfect bacon sandwich, even – on desperate, rainy days – a singing talent show with hairbrushes and the Top 40 on the radio. I was one of her Bluebells. My indigo sash still proudly hangs from the top of my wardrobe door.

The names of the girls from Gran's last camp are printed neatly down the page. I wonder if they still think of her. Her tinkly, mischievous laugh or her beady eyes. She could sniff a biscuit tin thief from miles away. She could make a daisy chain with her eyes closed. She was the best Gran.

Luckily I'm saved from a full-on weep by Susannah jangling the keys behind me.

'Home time! Or are you off to meet a fancy man?'

Steve is not what I'd call fancy. I'm not sure even Lucy would and she's legally obliged to compliment him. But he is my best mate, and it feels like he always has been.

He opens the door with scissors in hand, ever the teacher. I knew this Sunday roast invite came with a task attached: Steve's behind on the scenery he's making for *Fantastic Mr Fox*, the end of term show. He's craftily planned double-sided sets that can turn into a fox's den, a cornfield and a farmhouse kitchen in just a few clever twists. Steve has always been an inventor of sorts, starting with taking apart his remote control car at the age of eight and turning it amphibious. I mean, he tried to turn it amphibious. It's probably still at the bottom of Hazlehurst duck pond. And the ducks are probably still traumatised.

He went away to study product design at university but his plans had a bit of a redesign themselves as he met the love of his life Lucy and they made their own product, four-year-old Abel. So now he's back in his home village, retrained as a teacher, and fully immersed in life here. Thank cripes, because without him and Luce I would go completely nuts.

People always teased Steve and me about being Made For Each Other. Our birthdays are a week apart, we grew up next door to each other and we were always as thick as thieves when we were little. But as I get a glimpse of his builder's bum in his trackies, I'm reminded that I've never felt so much as a twinge of the hots for him, and I am so glad. I'd rather have a funny, reliable best friend than a terrible ten-minute fumble in 2003 to a Michael Bublé album. And I'm sure over the years, when I went through my various stages of wearing mega flares or beaded chokers or badly applied smokey eyes, he has not remotely fancied me either.

His hair is gelled, but his red curls refuse to take it lying down and are escaping into wispy question marks all over his head. The contrast in our colouring is what marked us out a mile away as a weird pair in secondary school: he's bright ginger and I am kohl black. It didn't help that I wore my hair long and unwashed and parted exactly in the middle. And that I played Massive Attack on loop in the common room, until the garage fans threw cans of Rio at my head.

Without asking, Steve pours red wine into a glass and presses it into my hands.

'I didn't want to ruin your weekend, so I didn't say anything at the time. But some bloke in a suit was in school on Friday. And a real suit, not the usual Asda job that we see round here.' He points at himself. 'He was asking when the last time we used Bluebell Hall for a school function was. And how many pupils would have attended. In exact numbers, Connie.'

All my nostalgic glow for the Attack vanishes, like someone had swapped that CD in my head for a *Greatest Hits* of Chris De Burgh.

'What? Why?!'

He shrugs. 'I didn't get that far. I just overheard him talking to Belinda on the desk, when I was restocking rulers. We did Roman centurions and it was a mistake on my part to pretend a metre stick was my sword. Hoping not to get any lawsuits, to be honest. But I think someone's sniffing around, about the Hall. You'd better work out what's going on. Before they do.'

I'm feeling so numb with worry that barely register my bum hitting the red gingham cushion on the kitchen chair. I'd been really looking forward to this roast, for ages, and now I felt like I'd already swallowed a bag of bowling balls. Usually I avoid being the third wheel to Steve and Luce's family time, as much as I can help it. Between lesson planning and assessing and marking and parents' evenings, he spends more time obsessing about other people's families than his own, which always grates on me. Let's not even get started on his paltry pay.

Lucy walks through the door, with Abel at her heels and a plastic bag on her wrist. 'Forgot the butter.' She clocks my face. 'Oh, you've told her. Steve, I said wait till after pudding, you berk.'

He puts his hands up in surrender. 'I cannot tell a lie. It's why you love me.' He opens the oven door and the delicious scent of roast chicken floods out, taking my mood from abysmal to only *mostly* abysmal.

'That, and you cook.' She bites down a smile.

'Lady!' Abel yells, and runs head-first into my thighs. You would think I hadn't seen him for three years, not three hours. This also has the result of perking me right up, taking me to a mere feeling of 'awful'. A miniature of his dad, Abel has called me Lady since he could talk – apparently he was once looking at a big photo of his first birthday party and Steve was pointing out everyone: 'There's your gran, there's your mum.' When he got to me, he said, 'There's Connie.'

'And she's a lady,' Abel said proudly. Steve's hysterical reaction to anyone calling me such a thing for the first time meant Abel gleefully said it forever and ever. But I don't mind. This kid is so sweet he could call me Dog Breath and I'd probably take it.

'So… Who do you think it is? An estate agent? A property developer?'

Steve wrestles a big dish of vegetable gratin onto the side, next to the resting chicken. It won't be all that rested when I'm finished with it. If I'm in the middle of an emergency, I'd better stock up on fuel. And booze. I knock back what's left of my wine and Luce seamlessly pours me some more.

'Couldn't get much more out of my network of spies, I'm afraid. Just: smart bloke, asking questions, taking notes. Pat thought he was cute, but then she would – she's a biology teacher. Randy,' he mouthed over the top of Abel's head.

Chairs are scraped back and glasses refilled as we sit down to eat. The food hits my plate and I confess just how bad the visitor numbers have been in recent months.

'And it's not as if I'm being complacent about it. I know the attendance is rubbish, it gives me indigestion sometimes.' I ignore Steve's snort of disbelief and continue to talk and eat at 100 miles per hour. 'I've tried so many things to get the Hall going, and they haven't worked. I knew I was in danger and that we by no means had 50 per cent of people coming but, well,' I shovel a forkful of cheesy broccoli deep into to my mouth, as if to bury my shame in greens, 'I just didn't think anyone was paying attention.'

Lucy nods and sips her wine. She's a quantity surveyor, and I know she's bitten her lip over the years when she's seen just how wobbly the Hall has become. But it also means she has a clear eye for a problem and assessing just how it can be fixed. 'OK. So we know someone is asking questions. But who? And why?'

'Mum,' Abel chips in excitedly, with his hand in the air, as if he's got all the answers, 'I don't know what you're talking about so can I watch Paw Patrol please?'

Smart kid.

'For one episode, then teeth and then bed, OK, sonny Jim?'

'OK, mummy Jim.' And he's gone in a blur of grey socks and muddy elbows. It's a relief, as I really don't want him to see a grown woman cry into a cheesy bake and a chicken leg.

'Could be someone from the estate, a harmless routine thing?' Steve suggests.

'But why wouldn't they just ring me?' I slap my hands to my forehead. 'Unless they don't trust me.

Unless they're getting ready to sack me. Oh god, they've probably done their sums and my P45 is in the post.'

'Well, hang on,' Lucy rubs my shoulder. 'If it's that severe then their lawyer probably would have come to see you directly, or asked to see the books. He'd be within his rights. So, it must be another interested party. Someone who…' As the thought hit her she broke off and became suddenly fascinated with pushing some carrots around her plate.

So I put her out of her awkward misery. 'Someone else who wants the Hall.' I knock back another glass of wine in one gulp. I must have taken out half their wine rack by now. I wish I was grown up enough to have a wine rack. I think they must come as standard with a marriage license and God knows I've got little chance of coming across one of those soon. 'So do you recommend teaching, Steve, or should I aim lower to be sure? I think they need a new sales assistant at the garage.'

'Cons, pull it together. Nothing is for definite yet. And no, do not become a teacher. The perks at the garage would be far superior. I hear they're getting a Costa machine. Come on, let's brainstorm how we get the Hall back on track.' He starts digging in his teacher bag for pens and paper. It's like Mary Poppins' carpet bag has swallowed up a Ryman's in there.

I use a bit of bread to sweep up the last of the gravy. There's something about gravy that reminds you the world must be a good place, if it's a world that could produce such a fatty, salty wonder sauce.

'OK, so I've tried reaching out to the baby brigade – put notices up for the Funday at the library and the GP. Had two new attendees today. They hated it.'

Steve scribbles down 'Tots' and puts a line through it immediately.

'Can't get the retirement home to visit again because of the leaky roof and that we don't have a ramp. Without proper health and safety regs, they aren't insured to be there.' I twiddle my fork as I talk.

'And the same goes for Hazlehurst Primary – we can't put on our plays there like we used to because it doesn't meet with safety checks. Plus, it's a bit small now the school's so much bigger than in Hibbs' day. Damn education for all, damn it!' I appreciate the effort he's making to keep things light. Old friends are the best for life saving silliness.

I plough on. 'I tried massage classes but that only attracted the slightly unsavoury locals.'

Steve writes down 'Massage – pervs' and puts a big cross by it.

'The yoga teacher I contacted said the Hall had a bad energy but I think it was actually the fact that she'd have to change in the kitchen, as we don't have any other rooms for that. The Bridge Club didn't last long because for the life of me I don't understand it, so I had no hope explaining the rules.' I finish the last of my food and wine. The comforting tastes and textures have helped relax me quite a bit, but despite the great loads of carbs now in my system, those bowling balls are still churning over in my stomach.

'I even went over Gran's old books for inspiration. But I just don't see flower arranging or hat decorating being a hit with villagers today. And I can't really afford to buy heaps of stuff for a class that might not go anywhere. And the teenagers absolutely won't come because you can't get 4G inside. Which, I'll admit, does suck.'

'So we know what the village doesn't want.' Steve points at the sad little list of my false starts. 'What we need to know is what they do want. Some market research. I remember that much from my product design days.'

I fiddle with my fringe as I think. I shouldn't – fine, flat black hair like mine needs no encouragement from chicken grease to go limp and lank. I'll look worryingly like my emo sixth form self again. 'I've got the Bluebells meeting coming up in a few days; I could corner the parents at pick up time, ask them what they think. I give them Tuesday nights without their kids, so they owe me.'

Steve puts down a Viennetta in the middle of the table. 'Which reminds me, Emo, if you want a big chunk of this we need to finish Mr Fox's house tonight and five styrofoam carrots. You give a little, to get a little.'

I swipe an errant chocolate flake from the table-cloth. 'Understood, sir.'

Chapter 2

I've lunged my way across the Hall, I've warmed up my arms with a 'Single Ladies' hand twist and now I'm ready for a Bluebells dance rehearsal. Trying to teach a gaggle of 6- to 12-year-olds how to do the same move pretty much involves doing it yourself a trillion times over. I've box-stepped so much over the last month that I'm almost confident I could give Davina McCall a run for her money. But as the girls will be dancing in the Easter parade, with all their family, friends, and any potential mean-name-callers from school watching, I want these girls to put their best dancing feet forward.

In years gone by we've made bonnets for Easter, as is traditional, but since I can't store anything in the Hall without it getting a sprinkling of black mould and most of the girls view glueing feathers and sequins onto things as a bit babyish, I've let it go. I had to bite my lip and not tell them that Lady Gaga has actually made a global empire out of gluing bonkers things onto her accessories – but then Beyoncé has made hers out of executing killer dance moves, so who knows which is a more sensible pastime. But the one thing I draw the line at is twerking. Not on my watch, Bethany Stevens, not on my watch. Gran would turn in her grave if she so much as knew twerking existed, let alone watched it go on down the high street.

So far we have a routine which is a little nineties Janet Jackson mixed with bits I've copied from *Britain's Got Talent* clips on YouTube. Lots of armography, lots of almost-on-time turns and jumps on the spot. We don't have a little enough girl to throw into the air and that's probably a blessing for everyone involved. It can't be too complicated a number, because we have to keep moving with the rest of the parade, but it has to be complicated enough to keep the girls busy for an hour every Tuesday from here until Good Friday. I'm saying lots of things I hope are helpful like 'Listen for the beat!' and 'Watch out for your neighbour's legs on the high kick!' And so far it's going pretty well. No squabbles and no broken ankles.

So take that, Mr Snoopy Suit, whoever you are, I think to myself.

The twenty-fifth playing of 'Beggin'' by Madcon finally ends. My ears do a happy wiggle to be free.

'Oh, can't we do it one more time?' Bethany asks from the back. 'I think I'm nearly getting that body roll.'

For the sake of Bethany and her next steps into puberty, I'm not going to let her perfect it for another week.

'Sorry! Here are your parents, though!' I trill. 'Everyone got their stuff? Bags and water bottles?'

Mums and dads start gathering at the open door. They never really come in – they've heard too much about the roof – but they're very glad for a free hour off a week. And these girls always surprise and delight me, so I'm happy for that hour too.

A small, chilly hand suddenly takes mine.

'Oh hello, Veronica. Are you ready? Is Mum here?'

'Yes, but first I'd like a word.'

I shouldn't have a favourite Bluebell, but I do, and it's Veronica. Really, she should be the Bloom Mistress – she's full of wisdom and poise, that one. She complimented me on getting my hair cut into a short bob last month, saying it gave me 'gravitas'. When I was 11 I would have said gravitas was Spanish for the little pebbles on your driveway.

Being the current Bloom Mistress gives me a weird kind of influence and responsibility and it still makes me want to laugh nervously. It wasn't all that long ago that I was perfectly at home crammed against other sweaty bodies at the front of the Pyramid Stage, drunk and dancing madly – it's a long way to the front of the queue at Homebase and other 'grown up' things. But I expect this stuff didn't come overnight to Gran, either, so I'm willing to learn on the job, even a few years in. I mean, I didn't have to fight off any other interested parties for the job, but I still feel like I'm 11 and covered in Care Bear stickers, never mind being a positive role model for the girls of today.

'OK. What's bothering you?'

'It's not me. I'm fine. It's you.' If she was a secret superhero in her spare time, she'd be Bank Manager Girl.

My eyebrows meet in the middle. 'What's wrong with me?'

'The girls are talking. They want to do a Taylor Swift song. They're Swifties. Many of them hadn't even started school when 'Beggin'' was out.'

I do the pop culture maths. She's right.

I lace my fingers together the way my Gran used to when she was buying time with children. 'Thank you for telling me. I shall see if I can get 'Shake It Off' to fit to the moves. How does that sound?'

Veronica narrows her eyes briefly. 'Acceptable. I'll tell the girls. Personally, I still find dancing in public a bit… unnecessary. But if it's for the good of the group, I'll carry on.'

I catch Veronica's mum's eye by the door and she shrugs as if to say 'Sorry for whatever grilling she's giving you, but I have to give her dinner every night so count your blessings.'

'Duly noted, Veronica. Goodnight.'

The girls file out, still with a rhythmic bounce to their steps, and I approach the earliest parents with a jovial hello, then leap into my questions about what services they might like to see run from the Hall. But all of a sudden I seem to have gone from cosy, free childcare to unbearably chipper chugger, because they all mumble about being late, and tea getting cold, and already doing so much... 'Anything I can do to make you happier at the Hall, let me know!' I singsong at their disappearing backs. 'Anything at all!' I think someone is about to turn around at that, when I realise it's a pervy single dad who turned up for the massage classes, so I quickly disappear myself.

I cross the room to get the broom (see, Mr Snoopy Suit, I am a great caretaker!). Five minutes later, it's just Gurpreet left, swinging her feet from a plastic chair.

'I'm sure Mum will be here soon, poppet.'

Gurpreet chews on the end of her long pony-tail, singing to herself. 'Yeah. Oh, actually it's Mrs Gooderson from next door who's coming. Cos Mum's working late. Yeah.' Gurpreet was one of those lovely dreamy girls you wish will never grow up and still be talking to trees and chasing birds when they're 23.

'What are you enjoying at school at the moment?'

'Lunch breaks.'

'Fair enough. And, Gurpreet love, is there anything you think we could do here at the Hall, anything that might people want to come more often?'

Desperate, yes, but she's still technically my market. The children are our future.

Gurpreet studies her shiny Clarks shoes.

'Do a lunch break?'

Well, it's been a long day for everyone. The sooner Gurpreet is on her way home, the sooner I can drag myself off and to bed and to some deep comatose sleep. Some of the school crew are getting together in the pub tonight, but I'm a bit too knackered to listen to their tracker mortgage woes right now.

A buggy rounds the doorway, followed by a familiar head of fire-engine red hair. 'Hello Mrs Gooderson!' Gurpreet skips over and tickles Sophie under the chin. Immediately she lets out a Fairy Liquid ad giggle. 'I can do my dance for you on the way home. Miss Duncan says we need to practise all. The. Time.' She starts busting out The Robot, much to Sophie's delight.

'Me again!' Flip gives that throaty cackle. 'Helping out my new neighbours with pick up, seeing as I work from home. Desperate to build up some babysitting brownie points. I haven't spent time with my husband without a baby wipe in view since… I think Gordon Brown was in power. Agh, I'm so old!' She pulls a comedy grimace.

How she has this much energy as the sun is setting, I have no idea. Whatever's in that red hair dye, I want some. Or maybe it's to do with her fitted scarlet cardi? I pull at my baggie sludge-colour hoodie with a niggle of shame making its way down my back.

'Before you go, could you just sign the log book for me? And date it Sunday? Sorry to be odd, but I forgot to ask you at the weekend. And attendance is so important to the Hall.'

I whip the book from the table by the door and flash it under her nose, biro jiggling alongside it.

'Shame you can't do something like sewing undies, really. I was talking about that to the WI ladies I've met, well the ones who don't switch their hearing aids off within five minutes of the meeting starting. They all seemed really keen.'

'All? How many was that?'

'I was talking to five or six girls. And I'm sure more would come once word got around.' Flip must have seen the creeping indecision as I bite the corner of my mouth. 'And I could help, you know. I have sewing bits, fabric offcuts. I have two great sewing machines I could lug here. If you maybe even did just one session, I could put the word about.' She raises her arch eyebrows a little higher.

'We'd need more than two machines, though. I wonder if the A-level college still does a Textile course?'

Flip nods quickly, jangling her earrings. 'Now you're talking!'

'They might lend us machines… And maybe the students would fancy it too? Something a bit more daring for the coursework portfolio.'

As she passes back the log book, I look at the reality of my situation: a short list of girls' names written in glittery pen, then Flip's below them in a barely legible scrawl. If the Hibbert estate demanded to see my books right now, which they are within their rights to do, I'd have almost nothing to show them – far from half of Hazlehurst bursting through my doors.

Gran might hate it, but then she'd hate losing the Hall even more. So much more.

I slap the book shut. 'I'm going to do it. We're going to do it,' I say with more courage than I feel. I can barely control a handful of Bluebells once a week;

how will I cope with adults armed with their own opinions and sharp scissors?

'Whoop!' Flip punches the air.

'Whoop!' Gurpreet joins in for kicks.

'Here's my number, doll.' Flip passes over a card. Philippa Gooderson, Digital and Social PR. 'Give me a call and we'll talk Liberty lawns and ribbons! See you.' She manages to air kiss and do a three-point buggy turn all at once. A proper PR person, now this could be interesting.

'Byeee Miss!' Gurpreet sings as she lunges her way down the path.

Knickers. Sewing knickers. Never mind Gran, what would poor old Puritan Hibbs think?!

–

When I get home, the lights are all off at 9.45 p.m. This means one of two things: Mum has already gone to bed, or Mum didn't get out of bed today. Since we lost Gran four years ago, Mum has found it really hard. She's always had 'black spots' as she used to call them, with a wry smile, times when her depression pulled her under and wouldn't let go. It started long before Mum and Dad split up when I was little, but of course that didn't help. And when Gran passed away, even though it was peaceful and quick, Mum tumbled again, without one of her supports in life. That's part of why I came back from Manchester. After graduating uni, I somehow sucked up to enough people to get a paid internship on a small music magazine in the city, *B-Side*. Though it was a small team, they all had big pretensions. At first, I think I saw it as a fun way to continue shouldering my way into the best, most exclusive gigs. And I certainly had no other inkling as to what to do with my degree. After a year I began to fancy myself a journo in the making, and wrote reviews in my spare time to gather a portfolio of work. Maybe one day I'd be such a prolific rock journalist that I could run my own festival? I had this idea of a festival that never set up in the same place twice and every year you'd have to wait with baited breath for our brightly-coloured flags to suddenly appear in your local park…

I was probably influenced in my ideas of fame and grandeur not just by the free tickets and t-shirts but also by Dell, one of the head writers. He was 28, had long blonde hair and smoked roll-ups. He pretty much came from the Rock and Roll Boyfriend textbook. Well, I thought he was my boyfriend. In my 22-year-old mind, at least, leaving a toothbrush and a spare pair of pants at the flat of someone you slept with every other night meant you were properly committed.

When I was twenty-three and had also squeezed a hairbrush onto Dell's bathroom shelf, a job as a junior writer came up. I thought it would be cute and bold of me to apply without telling him, emailing my portfolio to the editor when he had passed out asleep in front of *Match of the Day*. I had visions of us checking each other's work over brunch pastries and laughing at something droll Pete Paphides had written. Turns out I'm as good at reading men as I am at writing copy. Which is not good. Dell grabbed my hand the next afternoon and dragged me out of the office and into a dingy pub. I'll never forget the way his eyes narrowed when he asked me What the hell I was playing at, and Did I know what I'd done to his career?

When I spluttered in reply that I was just trying to make a career of my own he rolled those beady, narrowed eyes and said, Did I not get that I was an intern after two years for a reason? I just didn't have 'it', apparently. And the reference I'd made in one my reviews to him and I going to the same gig had now got him in serious trouble for sleeping with an employee.

'But we're not just sleeping together...' I started, but my voice dropped down to the sticky carpet and caught there. Dell looked anywhere but at me.

So I never went back to the *B-Side* office after that. I left my stapler on my desk and my spare pants at Dell's. I registered with a temping agency the next day and spent a couple of years working for parts manufacturers, accountants – I even temped for a week at a Freemason lodge. My only stipulation was that I wouldn't write copy, of any kind. I worked hard, I had fun with my uni mates who had stuck around too and I put all my energies into being feckless and young. At least I knew I was good at that.

Besides, I always had half an idea that I'd go back to Hazlehurst one day, if I'm honest. Not necessarily to do Gran's job, but Mum has always needed me in a special way. I don't feel resentful, or angry, or disappointed. I love my mum, and I want to help her if I can. Moving in after Gran passed just made loads of sense. We're the only two left in our family now, and we Duncans stick together. And the further I was from Manchester and *B-Side* and the chance of ever bumping into Dell in a noisy bar back then, the happier I was.

I touch the framed picture of Gran that sits on the hall table, by the dusty telephone. 'Almost there, Gran, the girls are nearly on the beat. And there are no shoulder shimmies, you'll be pleased to hear. But the lightbulb went in the loo again so I'm going to have to brave that tomorrow.' I'm almost on the verge of telling her about the new sewing class idea but I stop myself. Bonkers to keep a secret from a photograph of a woman in a twin set, but that's the truth of it.

The answerphone light is blinking so I hit the play button. 'Hello Jane, hello Connie. Just wondering how you both are, and if you fancied Sunday lunch soon, at The Pheasant? They have a new chef apparently. We could go and do our best Gregg Wallaces. Anyway, let me know what you think.'

It's one of Mum's oldest school friends, testing the waters, seeing how she's faring. Our friends have been so good to both of us in the last few years. Living somewhere as small as Hazlehurst might not be glamorous and super cool and full of theatres or sushi bars with those little conveyor belts, but it is full of people we know and people who love us.

'Good night?'

'Holy crap! Mum, you scared me!'

She takes a careful step down the stairs and reaches the bottom. 'Stop being dramatic. If I'd wanted to scare you, I would have thrown myself down from the top.'

'That's not funny.' I wag a finger in her direction.

Mum scratches her hair. It looks pretty clean, which is a good sign for today. 'If you think about it, it is funny. In a black humour kind of way. But I can happily report I went to work today. Budgens had

one of the world's finest price ringers back on duty.'
Though she has her lips pressed together, I know she's
feeling really glad about that.

As it seems to have been a less rocky day than most,
I'm going to risk asking the thing that was turning
around in my head the whole walk home.

'Mum, do we still have Gran's old electric sewing
machine? And would you mind if I borrowed it?'

–

I honestly had every intention of an early night.
But here I am at 2.13 a.m., on the sofa, accidentally
digging pins into my thighs, as my old Take That
tour t-shirt keeps riding up when I take big pulls
of my needle and thread. (OK, so I wasn't always
an emo teen. Mark Owen's cheeky smile held my
heart long before black nail varnish and My Chemical
Romance.) I woke up halfway through a dream that
I was sitting my Textiles GCSE but when I started
to make the kitchen apron I'd planned, I opened the
paper pattern and it was a ball dress. With a corset
and a tulle skirt and everything. I had that drooping
feeling of not having done any homework and was
waiting for the teacher to boom 'Connie Duncan
you have FAILED' just as I jerked awake. So rather
than go back to that dream, and since I turned out
all of Gran's sewing stuff with Mum earlier tonight, I

thought I should make a start on the Bluebells' Easter parade outfits. It's just blue shorts that the girls had to bring from home (with a leotard underneath) and I'm sewing a little patch with our Bluebell emblem onto the bottom right-hand side. Both Mum and Susannah have said they could help, but I'm happy doing it on my own. Even if my stitches are far from neat and even. I look like I'm trying to sew Frankenstein up in a bit of a hurry.

When I'd first woken up at just before one, I'd turned to my old friend Phone Scrolling to shut my mind down, but the opposite happened, which it always does. It's a bad friend, if I'm honest. A few drunken messages from the school guys out for drinks, calling me out for 'being a bad egg' and then mysteriously sending me random Craig David lyrics. Facebook was a mixed bag. I still followed the page for *B-Side*, from back when I'd set it up as an intern and seen the very first Like. I think it was a mix of pride at the 10,000-odd followers now and that dark kind of self-loathing where you want to see how great an ex is looking in holiday photos and badger yourself to exhaustion over it. So now and again it would pop up in my feed, a big interview with Chris Martin leaving a sting behind my ribs that was in no way lovely Chris's fault. And it wasn't the magazine's fault, either, I'd chide myself – it wasn't their fault that I simply wasn't cut out for that world. Or that my ex was a pillock. At least it had taught me a lesson about knowing my limits and not falling for pretentious men who spent more time archiving their vinyl collections than chatting to real humans.

Facebook was also telling me to look back on stuff that happened on this very day and it seems eight years ago today I had a scrubbed-fresh face, leaning forward at a big pub table, a stupid grin on my face that could only have been put there by cider, and I was with my big gang of uni mates. Claire, Simon, Tallie, Vickers, Hungry Dave. All the Wainwright Road peeps. My crew.

It was such an awesome picture of us, young and bright-eyed and wearing questionable asymmetrical tops, that I hit Share before I really thought about it. And within minutes I got a ping from a comment.

Oh god this has cheered up my night feed! I'm sure it's going to be the first of many with this hungry little dude. Can I go back and have my student sleep days again please?!?! wrote Claire.

And then another ping soon after: *Sleep is for wimps! I miss that cheap cider, though. It's the one thing you can't find in New York (winky face).* From Simon. I had heard his law firm had sent him out on secondment there. All his photo posts were of hotdogs and steaming air vents these days, jammy sod.

As I give myself a third thumb prick and snap off a thread, I realise being up on New York time isn't going to do good things for me tomorrow, with this new evening class to arrange in a hurry. So, using the light from my phone – still showing my beloved flashback picture – I carefully climb the stairs to bed and the Mark Owen bedspread waiting for me.

Chapter 3

Going through some of Gran's old sewing bit and pieces was a really lovely thing for Mum and me, though I'd imagined it would be like poking a recent wound. Gran wasn't big on sewing – I think it was a bit sedentary for her and you couldn't go off piste that much, you had to follow the patterns. But she had enjoyed making costumes for the kids in the family or for the Bluebells when need arose, because costumes could be silly and flimsy and fun, and it didn't matter if the hem was at a 45 degree angle.

There wasn't much in her sewing box beyond some scraps of fake fur and a few ribbons, but I had my eye on those. Her sewing machine was a real corker, though: it was pistachio green, a gorgeous sixties affair, with sleek lines and all manner of gizmos. Electric too, so at least that meant I wouldn't develop one manly arm from turning a handle over and over. I wouldn't go so far as to say Gran would have approved of me whipping up knickers with her stuff, but she would have agreed that anything was a worth a try if it came down to keeping Bluebell Hall up and running.

On Wednesday I'd made some fliers and persuaded Steve to photocopy them for me at school, when the head, Mrs Simmons, wasn't around. These went up on the village noticeboards, in the cafe window, at the doctor's surgery and anywhere else locally that I knew had a friendly patron or Bluebell parent at the helm.

Time for some big kid fun?
Fancy learning to sew?

Come along to a FREE taster session of sewing classes where we'll be learning to make a small something for ourselves, with plenty of ribbons and bows. Email ConnieTheHall@gmail.co.uk to book your place. Friday 2nd April, 7.30 p.m. till 9 p.m. Drinks and crisps included!

I emailed it round to the list of addresses I had from the visitors' book. The first thing I did when I took over at the Hall was to annotate the 'address' column with a big 'EMAIL' but I can't blame Gran for not thinking of that. She thought YouTube was a kind of superglue, after all.

Speaking of YouTube, or a few days now I've been watching video clips back to back like an tween obsessive – I've found loads of helpful sewing tutorials. Searching for 'knickers at home' on my first go was a monumental mistake, and I needed a stiff drink and to scrub my eyeballs after those results popped up. But I had a go at a pair myself and they didn't come out half bad: black and white polka dot cotton with a turquoise trim. They were probably an excellent fit for a 14-year-old, once I'd trimmed off the wonky bits for the fifth time. But they were knickers. And quite cute if I say so myself. It brought back some of my Textiles GCSE lessons, though thankfully not that dream again. That said, I'm not sure a pair of thin knickers with a ribbon tie at the side would have got me better than my own C grade. It probably would have got me a letter home and a visit from a social worker.

We'll have to share a few machines for our first session – I'm going to charm the college for more when we have one good class under our belts. Or under our knicker elastic, I should say. But Stevie has come up trumps in the back of his school's old Home Ec room (now an IT lab, of course) and found three pairs of dressmaking scissors, still crazy sharp from underuse, a few tape measures and a box of old pins. This, together with the bits Flip is bringing, a few trestle tables, some jaunty tablecloths, a punch bowl of kettle chips and all the will in my world, would make our first Sew Your Own Knickers night. Bring it on, Mr Snoopy Suit. I'm not taking this lying down.

A familiar face gives me a big shock as I'm waiting for the class to show up. 'Susannah! You're here!'

'Of course I am, dear.' She smooths her charcoal grey pencil skirt underneath her and sits on a plastic stacking chair. 'I've brought my own sewing kit, to boot.'

'But you said hells bells to it!'

She blinks coolly at me. 'No, Constance. You asked me what Rosemarie would have said, and I told you. But I will support whatever you do to meet new people, and try new things.'

'For the good of the Hall.'

'Yes, that too. Besides, I remember your GCSEs, and that apron. I thought you might need some help.'

Why hadn't I thought of it before? Susannah was a card-carrying old lady with all the handicraft skill that went with it – she'd be a whiz on Gran's machines and could make sure I wasn't using bias binding instead of elastic, as I had in my first abysmal attempt.

'Well, I'm very happy to have you here. Can I get you tea while we wait for the others? I have five definites and I hope some drop-ins. More next week if it all goes to plan and Flip can help spread the word.'

As I'm boiling the kettle for two teas, I hear our PR guru clatter in lightly on heels, put down something with a clunk (I'm guessing her sewing machine) and launch into a conversation with Susannah about how she started sewing. She's running through the courses she's taken, from adult evening classes to an intensive week at the WI college, as I come back in with the drinks. I had no idea such a place existed but it sounds pretty cool. 'My mum absolutely hated anything close to a domestic science!' she hoots. 'But in her defence, she was a radical. It just screamed oppression and stupefaction to her. To me, it just means half an hour of headspace and clothes that actually fit my breasts!'

Neither of us can now help but look at Flip's impressive bosoms, clad in what must be a hand-knitted pea-green cardigan.

She's thundering on, really enjoying her subject. I just get the impression Flip enjoys everything to the maximum, and I love that about a person. Gran used to say 'some people are drains and some people are radiators. The drains just suck up everything good that comes their way and all they do is give back a bad feeling in return. But radiators make a place more comforting, they make people feel warm and welcome. Some people can't help being drains but it doesn't mean you have to fill your house with them.'

I tune back into Flip's chatter. 'But any skills women can teach women are a joy, and an essential part of how we shore up the generational relationships, stay strong as a community, share our strengths and cover our weaknesses. That's why I was so keen to join the WI when I moved here. And when it comes to sewing, well, my daughter Melody and I might row about the Wi-Fi code – I reset every day at 10 p.m.,' she nods conspiratorially, 'but we can come together over making her a prom dress from scratch. And it's much cheaper to boot!' Cackle cackle.

'There is something special about being in the company of women, almost sacred.' Susannah nods.

And that's just when Dominic arrives.

–

I'm feeling like some sort of Stone Age idiot right now; it's a wonder I can summon the mental energy to make two more cups of tea in the tiny kitchen. But it's the perfect place to hide the red shame burning through my cheeks. Can't hide forever, though. This tea won't deliver itself.

When I read Dom's email last week I just assumed it was short for Dominique, because the email mentioned bringing a daughter and wanting to try out sewing for a while. So my mind went to a woman. Not a man. And, besides, I kind of was unthinkingly advertising the class to women, it being about making undies.

Blimey, but he can't have worked that out. I didn't want to put 'knickers' specifically on my flier, having learnt the hard way that you don't want the more letchy residents involved in something like this, and I didn't want any sweet old ladies at the library to have a heart attack, either. But clearly I'd been far too subtle. Because here was Dom, in a rugby shirt, his frowns sending thick ripples through his forehead, looking completely out of his depth as it was. I think if I show him the pants pattern he might just wither into a small lump of polyester and chinos. And forget Dom's discomfort for a minute; how can I happily teach a minor to make frilly undies!?

His daughter, Polly, has definitely inherited his olive-y complexion but she already stands over him by half a foot, and can only be in her mid-teens. Their body language is eerily in sync, though, twitchy and unsettled, shifting in their seats, toying with cotton reels and bias binding. I think they want to be here but they're clearly very scared too. Then it hits me – Polly is the teen that called the Sunday Funday lame and stormed out. This is what you call a tough customer.

So I'm thinking on my feet. What else could we make? It has to be easy. Because my skills are average at best. Not use much fabric. Because we don't have much, just a handful of decent pieces Flip has magic-ally dug from her supplies. Be altogether PG-rated, teen-level cool AND man-friendly. I flick my eyes around the Hall, desperate for a bit of inspiration. If only we had 4G around here so I could pilfer a craft blog on the sly. I so need everyone to think I'm in charge here…

The noticeboard isn't telling me much; the windows are bare but I think curtains are way beyond me; a draft excluder for the door maybe? God, that's depressing. We need something fun, something cheery. I need a good thought right now. I can't think about losing the Hall, all Gran's hard work, another disappointment for Mum…

I blink a few times and look up at the ceiling, hoping the early tears hanging about will disperse.

And there it is: two triangles of bunting. In the very far right-hand corner, two triangles of paper bunting with the Union Jack printed on them, left there from – possibly the Jubilee party? We must have ripped it all down the next day but not noticed that last bit. For once, my amateur caretaking has paid off!

'Bunting!' I clap my hands and yell so brightly that Susannah spills a little of her tea.

'Ooooh lovely!' Flip pulls her chair into the table, eyeing up my ribbon supplies. She's looking between

Dom, Polly and myself and clearly working out this is something not to question, but just to go with.

'This is a class in how to make bunting!' I continue cheerily. Can't be too hard, I think, triangles and a stringy bit. Right sides together. Not hard. Not sexist. That'll do, Miss Duncan.

'That sounds good, doesn't it, pet?' Dom nudges Polly in the ribs with his elbow. She doesn't reply.

I shove the pattern pieces I'd carefully traced way down into my handbag and root about for my Filofax instead. Good old Filofax, you may be mocked, you may well deserve to be left behind in the days of giant mobile phones and shoulder pads, but I love you. And, crucially, you have your little ruler for emergencies like this. 'I'm just going to… Fetch the triangle templates from… The kitchen, where I've been storing them. In the meantime, have a rummage through the fabric to find two pieces you think would make a good triangle bit.'

'A pennant,' Susannah offers.

'Exactly!'

When I come back with three triangles – the most I could get from the giant cardboard box of tea under the sink – the classmates are sharing scraps silently. It might not be a riot of conversation and neighbourly bonding just yet, but they are working together, at the very least. And that's a start.

'OK! So we'll draw round this template twice, on the wrong side of the fabric. We can use a bog standard biro, it won't matter as we're turning it inside out before we fix it all together.'

Polly's glossy red lips are puckered together. Oh boy. 'We don't have much fabric here, do we? I mean, like, for actual bunting that is supposed to be long and junk?'

I force out a bubbly laugh. 'Oh, of course we don't. We're just focusing on technique today, and next time we can talk more about complementary colours, forming patterns, that sort of thing. So, Flip, Susannah, once we have drawn our triangles, I wondered if you might show the others how to sew them up on the machine?'

Flip's eyes gleam as she eyes up new local friends in the making. Outsourcing rocks. I'm muddling about with an idiot's level of understanding, when I have two mega sewers right here. Flip is especially quite clearly happy to be the Hermione to my Ron. But without the unresolved romantic tension. Susannah is like a McGonagall in better threads. And I can keep everyone's drinks and crisp quota full and get the conversation flowing.

'So Polly,' I lean over her to put down another bowl of sea salt and vinegar, five minutes later. 'What did you like the look of?'

'Um, these stripes. A thin red one and chunkier blue one. We… I really love Devon so they make me think of beach huts and deck chairs.'

Susannah points one delicate finger at the two carefully drawn triangles. 'That is a lovely combination. Very classic, very chic.'

'Um, thank you.' Polly seems to hide most of her face behind her long burgundy-dyed hair and tries not to let her smile show.

'Being creative is so good for the soul!' Flip fizzes with energy. She's like tipping a packet of sherbet into some flat Coke. 'The only creative outlet I get most days is choosing which dino t-shirt to combine with which pair of brown cords for my son. Which is academic anyway as within two minutes he has grass stains rubbed into at least one of those!'

The stress creases in Dom's forehead are thankfully disappearing. He looks like an uncle who's just been allowed off the dance floor at a family wedding, and has re-joined his quiet pint at the back of the do. He must be in his mid-forties but has the air of someone older, and much more weary than his years. He clears his throat and joins in. 'My Polly here used to hate any kind of mess – if she was in the garden she wanted to wash her hands every five minutes, if she got so much as a splash of milk on her top we'd have to change into an entirely new outfit. And a matching one, of course.' Flip and Susannah nod with aplomb so I think I might as well match them. It's only Polly who remains unmoved.

'That was, like, ages ago, Dad,' she says in a tiny voice. 'So embarrassing.'

He sucks in his cheeks and continues less confidently. 'Yes, well. You certainly are different about mess now, if your room is anything to go by. Hoards socks like they're going out of fashion.'

'How can socks be fashionable, Dad? Omigod!' Polly gets up and storms off, her trainers slapping on the dusty parquet.

'I'll just give her a minute.' Dom looks down at his hands, moving his thumbs round and round in fast circles.

Flip leans forward slightly in her chair. 'Tough having to be the bad guy, isn't it? My husband was all for sleep training our daughter, as long as it was me that did the crying bits!' She smiles kindly at our solo male sewer.

He draws his hands down his face and lets out a puff of breath. 'I'm bad guy, I'm good guy, I'm homework guy. I'm… I'm it. It's just me now. We lost Polly's mum when she was nine. So, I'm just trying my best.' He shrugs. 'The first few years were fine, she only wanted me, we stuck together. But now… Now I'm enemy number one. That's why I thought this would be good, do something a mum might do, spend time together when I'm not having to shout at her over the ironing pile.'

'You poor soul.' Susannah puts down her scissors and pats him on the back of the hand.

'Shit,' Flip mumbles.

I clear my throat and approach Dom. No wonder he looks so world-weary. 'You've done exactly the right thing coming here – and not just to share an interest with Polly, but because now you've found a new support group, new friends.'

There's a croak from Dom's throat; I think maybe he's bitten back a sob. 'Sorry, I've never said these things before, and now they've just come pouring out. What's in this tea, eh?' He tries to laugh gruffly.

I give him the briefest of shoulder squeezes. He has a look in his eye that I've seen in my mum before, during her dark days. 'Better out than in. Do you want to go and see if she's OK now? And next week, I promise I will think of a way to make it a bit more cool for Polly, make her an integral part of the group. And you too, Dom!'

I have no idea how I'm going to achieve this but there's a steely feeling in my chest that tells me I won't give up till I work it out. Because that's just what Gran would do.

Chapter 4

All good planning needs a bun to kickstart it, and luckily Hazlehurst has the best finger buns known to man, at Crusty's bakery at the bottom of the high street. So with Dom's words still echoing round my head and a fresh bun at my side, I'm back at work on a Saturday morning. There was nothing but cobwebs in my social calendar, anyway. After enough lame excuses, my old school friends have stopped inviting me to nights out in protest, and Steve is now more of a seven-letter-word-in-Scrabble guy than a monosyllabic, grunting drunk guy on your average Saturday night. I haven't been to a real gig in years, or a festival. I can't even remember where I keep my glitter gel and airbed, to be honest. But now I have my sewing night not just as a way to help bring new visitors to my little shack but also bring some calm to a family in turmoil, it's my wholehearted focus. Anyway, I'd much rather be thinking about the Hall on a Saturday morning than inspecting the maker's mark on my toilet bowl.

I'm humming as I do a quick check on the kitchen at the Hall, and its supplies. It could have waited till Monday morning but I was so buzzing with what our little party of five could turn into that I was too twitchy to stay home and read or get into a Netflix box set. I wanted to be at the place where it all happens, where friends can be made over a box of pins and some home truths. It's exactly why the Hall has to live on for the village – Dom and Polly were living just a handful of streets away and yet no one knew how hard they were having it. None of us knew that a family was struggling next door, unhappy and unsure how to make things better. But by coming out and meeting us, Dom now has three new people on his side. Three friends that have his corner. And I'm not letting go of this place without a big old fight.

So we have plenty of tea bags, could do with more sugar. Some of these mugs have brown rings so stubborn it looks like I've been serving up hot Ronseal. I could probably chuck them and bring in some from home, it's not like Mum and I need more than four mugs at any one time anyway. Hands on hips, I do a sweeping stare around the kitchen. It's small but in relatively good nick, compared to the main hall itself. I could give it a lick of paint, you know. Fill in the cracks, sand them down. Find some sealant stuff for the damp patches, as a temporary fix. There's a big bucket of brilliant white in the garage. It might not get Sarah Beeny in a lather but it would certainly brighten things up. The last time I painted something was… my first house share in Manchester, post-uni. Years ago now. We'd begged the landlord to let us go over the terracotta orange which somehow managed to be both dull and eye-watering. He was very glad we were doing the graft for him. And though I'm lacking cash right now, I do have endless supplies of graft.

My DIY skills might be patchy but if YouTube could teach me to make pants it could certainly remind me how to slap some emulsion on. I could dig out some brushes tomorrow, in fact, make a start, be ready for the Bluebells on Tuesday…

The brass letter box gives a loud metallic clap and I jump out of my skin. Post? We never have post here. I jog round to the front door and scoop up a thin white envelope from the floor. Hibbert Estates is stamped neatly in the top left.

Oh no.

I crane my neck to look through the thin window just by the front door. It's a bit murky (cleaning windows is at the bottom of my list) but I can just see the glint of sunshine bouncing off a pair of classy grey suit trousers as they get into a shiny car, and drive away.

Oh no, no, no.

–

At the duck pond I'm flapping more than a Hazlehurst mallard after a dropped panini. But a toasted sarnie can't help me – I'm in a right tailspin.

'They want to inspect our records in 30 days. 30 days! That's… in May!' I shake my wrists frantically like I've just put my hand in a spider's web. 'They're going to know and they'll take the Hall and I'll be sacked and the Bluebells will be homeless! The OAP choir will have no reason to live, the Carter boys will run wild in the village. It'll all go tits up!'

Steve points to the space next to him on the bench. 'Not too close to the water, buddy!' he yells over to Abel, who is having a long talk with one very nosy duck about his favourite sandwich fillings. 'Be still. Sit. Deep breath. Firstly, the Bluebells all have real homes and they can do synchronised dances to Katy Perry just about anywhere.'

'Taylor Swift,' I correct him, to which he replies with that withering teacher look of exhaustion.

'Anyway… Nothing's happened yet. It's all to play for. A lot can happen in 30 days. You had new visitors last night, right? So that's something.'

'But only three. And it's not enough.' I pull my long purple jumper over my knees and pick at my cuticles. I can hear Abel clearly stating that you should never try egg salad, even if you're starving.

Steve's tufts of ginger curls bounce in the breeze. 'We worry that you're doing too much on your own, Connie. Luce and I, that is. You're trying to save the Hall, you're looking after your mum. When do you do things, I don't know, just for fun?'

A prickle of annoyance goes up my neck. I really don't need this conversation again. I blow out my cheeks. 'Well, when do you? You work and you have Abel to look after and you and Luce never get to go out, beyond the rare occasion you take me up on babysitting!'

He laces his fingers together. 'That's different.'

'How?'

But I know how. And I know he doesn't want to say it, because he's a good friend. It's different because they have each other. And they have Abel. I try to swallow but my throat has gone tight.

'I'm not trying to wind you up, Connie.' He leans his square shoulder against me, almost tipping me over and I can't help but break into a laugh. 'I just think you don't have to go it alone. Not always. It's totally fine to ask for help. Don't you always say that's why you love the Hall? It brings people together.'

To: Susannah; GoodersonPR@gmail.co.uk;
dom2272@yahoo.co.uk
From: Connie Duncan

Hi guys,

So lovely to meet on Friday! I was wondering if anyone could meet on Monday night too?

I have a problem and I would really really love your help. I'll bring the biscuits if you bring the brainpower.

Connie the Caretaker X

–

Mum had a good day today and baked me some flapjacks. They're sitting proudly in the centre of the table, the centrepiece to a feast of sewing supplies. Last week we actually managed to get the pennants sewn into relatively even triangles, so I suppose this time we should have a go at joining them all up with bias binding. Bias binding always makes me think of one of those ancient rules of law, like habeas corpus, but after a quick Google of my knicker prep I found it actually just means bias as it's cut at a 45 degree angle, thereby making it nice and flexible. As Steve says when he gets a new teacher in school, fresh faced and armed with binders of lesson plans, 'All the gear but no idea' – and if he's really tired 'All the kit but most likely shit'. I'm learning all I can about sewing up bunting but it doesn't mean my top stitching won't be rubbish. But then again, I now know what top stitching actually is! That's progress.

As my bunting team file in and arm themselves with hot drinks and buttery snacks, I blurt out the whole shebang: how Hibbs left the Hall to the village for life, unless it wasn't being used by enough of the population. And now it isn't, and the estate is onto us. I finish with a bitter reference to Saville Row tailoring and Cold War spies.

Dom holds a finger in the air. 'Hang on a tic, before we worry. What's the appeal process?'

'Huh?' I wind some purple thread round and round my wrist until it starts to bite.

'I have a franchise that I bought from a big restaurant chain.'

Polly fake coughs next to him but clearly says between comedy splutters, 'Chicken shop.'

'Yes, but… OK! I had to do lots of contract work and reading the fine print. When it comes to properties already in use, there are usually loads of appeal processes, exception clauses, at least processes where you can slow things down a bit while you catch your breath. Do you have any sort of tenancy contract, anything like that?'

'It might be in with Gran's stuff about the Hall. I started to go through it when I took on the place, but it got a bit upsetting to rifle through her bits and bobs if I'm honest.'

Polly shuffles her shoes about under the table and blinks her eyes. I might have hit on something too close to home.

Dom lays his arm behind Polly's chair but she leans forward, away from him. 'Bring in what you've got, for Friday. I can have a look, for what it's worth.'

'Oh Dom, you beauty!' If he didn't look so much like my old French teacher, I would kiss him. This feels like the first glimmer of sunshine that's made it through the Bluebell Hall patchy roof in ages. Maybe we could find just a few more months, just a bit more time.

Flip blows on her tea with such force I'm worried most of it will end up on Susannah's suede loafers. 'Obvs you can count on the WI joining our group, as of this Friday.'

'Really!? All of them?'

'Yup, all 15 local members. Which means we'll need more sewing machines. I could bring my spare, see if the ladies could bring theirs? Can't hurt.'

Before I can thank her, she's taken a big breath and she's off again. 'We need to get the story out there. In my London life, I was a PR for digital start-ups but PR is PR. It's about saying the right things at the right time, usually while you plaster everyone with booze. And who has the ear of everyone in the village?'

I shrug stupidly. 'Mr Singh the pharmacist?'

'No!' I get a 100 miles per hour eye roll from Flip. 'The Village Committee! They organise the May Day fete, the Easter parade, village of the year competitions, the open garden days. They can literally get the whole of Hazlehurst in one place with a click of their fingers and a dozen free scones. At least, that's what I hear via my WI spies.'

I think I'd rather ask Mr Singh for help, even if it's just for a good migraine tablet. 'But they gave up on the Hall as an eyesore years ago. They just ignore my emails for help, every time.'

Susannah readjusts her long jade necklace. 'Then we won't ask for something. We'll offer something.'

My clueless mug is all Susannah needs to go on. 'It's better to beg forgiveness than ask permission, dear. I say we make enough bunting for the Village fete, metres of the stuff, and we present it to them without asking whether they need it or not. I've lived in this village for decades and the one thing locals hate is an awkward situation. So they'll say thank you very much and they'll have to start paying attention to the Hall again.'

I nod furiously. 'Yes – I remember that year we had two cake tents at the fete because the mayor at the time was too embarrassed to tell Gran she should leave the WI to it. That was the start of the beef between them, really. You and I are like Hazlehurst's very own Romeo and Juliet, born to warring families.' I nod at Flip.

Her laugh erupts loudly. 'I hope we come to better ends! I'm all for hundreds of metres of bunting – you could wrap me in the stuff as far as I'm concerned – but my fabric haul won't cover all that. Where will we get the resources?'

Resources are something I'm short on – Gran's leftover ribbony bits won't stretch around the park. They probably wouldn't stretch around the goal posts.

Susannah wrinkles her neat lips. 'I can raid the rag bag at the hospice shop, when I do my shifts. You get some lovely cotton shirts and such in there, which we can't sell because of iron burns or stains. I'm sure my neighbours have old haberdashery supplies they could part with. Most of the old dears there don't have the eyesight to sew these days.' She says 'old dears' like she's there to serve them tea, whereas really she's now one of the oldest residents at the retirement home. 'And we could go out, asking for donations.' Her eyes sparkle for a brief moment. 'Maybe we make it in the village colours, if we can swing it. And then once the committee are feeling gracious and touched, we offer them a plan of how they'll be our knights in shining armour. Once they're buttered up.'

'Bunting-ed up!' Polly forgets her teenage snarl for a moment in the face of a good pun.

Dom laughs that bit too loud in support and immediately kills the mood, bringing back her snarl with a vengeance. Poor Dom.

A sudden burst of energy has me pacing back and forth, my sparkly trainers squeaking on the parquet. 'Guys, let's do this. First up: I'll get the paperwork to Dom. Susannah and Flip can start selecting fabrics and cutting them down. We'll soon be joined by the WI army and all the Singers they can muster. And Polly—' The reedy girl flinches as I say her name, like she's been busted on her phone in third period Physics. 'Polly, I would really like you to be my design consultant on this. Once we have the pennants ready, will you arrange them in the best pattern you can come up with? I can tell you've got an eye for style, your clothes are always cool.' I hope young people are still saying cool. I hope she doesn't look at my Sainsbury's leggings and long flannel shirt and decide I am no way eligible to even use the word 'cool'.

Polly wraps her hands around the base of her neck, as if to hide the blush starting there, or – hopefully not – the beginning of a gag mime. 'Me?' she half-whispers.

'Of course. If this bunting is going to hang around the village, it's got to look… on fleek.'

'Um, sure. Yup. OK.' I think in teen lingo that passes for excitement.

Dom beams beside her like a torch suddenly switched on.

I fold my arms. 'Then we're set. Bluebell bunting is go!'

Chapter 5

There's not a cloud in sight for the Easter parade, which is a godsend because last year we had the wettest egg hunt on record and little Bryan Malone accidentally bit into a muddy pine cone, thinking it was a really soggy chocolate egg.

Mum didn't really feel energetic enough to face the crowds today, so it's just me keeping up a 'Shake It Off' beat as the girls limber up behind the starting line. Some rogue red nail varnish has been sneakily applied but it's too bright and sunny for me to tell anyone off today. And those Bluebells rules about no cosmetics were written in 1953 so I'm going to postdate with a bit of feminism and say: it's your body. Paint it how you like.

Mum has set herself the task of washing and sorting our walk-in linen cupboard, though, while I'm out. It used to be called the lounge but now we're taking in rag bag donations from Susannah and stacks of old tablecloths and fine lawn shirts and linen napkins from across the village, there's barely room for a scatter cushion, let alone any actual lounging by humans. I've heard her make the odd grumble about 'not being a laundry, thank you very much' but we've also loved a wee bit of snooping into what people pass on. It seems Mr Aldridge has one sharp elbow, because he donated a bin bag full of work shirts all sporting the same hole in the left sleeve. Does he sharpen it or something? And Mrs Alridge followed him up the drive with another bin liner, this time 'full of things his mother gave me.' By the look of the antimacassars embroidered with woodland sprite scenes therein, they don't seem to share the same tastes.

Chopping up pixies on cloth is for tomorrow. Today is for choppy pixie bobs, in honour of T Swift. I have tried to give my own bob a bit of attitude with a squeeze of mousse but it's still doing its Wednesday Addams thing. Nevermind, I'm just the ringmaster in this whole affair – the girls are the real show. And their blue shorts are a vision of matching loveliness, even if the Bluebell badges are all sewn in slightly different degrees of neatness. These girls are what this village is all about.

'Bluebells, are you ready?'

'Yes, Mistress Bloom!'

'I can't hear you. Are you ready?'

'YES!'

'Nope, can't hear that. Are you READY?!'

Just as the girls are shrieking at their loudest, Veronica steps forward. 'Miss, have you had your hearing looked at? Because we really are being very loud. Or is this a motivational thing?'

'Motivation. All done now, thanks Veronica. Let's get dancing!' I yell.

There's a ringing of an old-fashioned clapper bell, and off we go. Just half a mile of coordinated dance moves with the full village watching. Piece of cake.

–

I should have known it would be Bethany Stevens. Instead of pivot, grapevine, double clap and back again, she didn't go back again but instead waved madly at her mum, allowing Gurpreet to grapevine into her and Veronica to high kick into Gurpreet. And instead of a fluid, choreographed number taking us past the bakery and the stationer's and along to the church where we could be rewarded with luke-warm squash, I ended up detangling limbs and being rewarded with red-hot public shame.

'Ow! Miss! My arm!'

'My ankle!'

'My eyebrows!'

I clamp my hands by my sides, wobbling a bit with fury. 'Bethany, how have I hurt your eyebrows?'

She rolls her eyes. 'You reached past me to get Gurpreet's leg off of Charlene's plait and you smudged my brow line.'

The local am dram float is overtaking us, even in their bulky Shakespearian neck ruffs, seeing as we've caused a backlog in the procession. We are to this parade what a lorryload of spilled marbles would be to the M25.

I can see the fire truck not far behind, two of the area's firemen walking along beside it, shaking buckets of loose change and throwing some loose smiles into the crowds for good measure. If I wasn't in my dowdy Bloom Mistress gear of blue culottes and polo shirt, I could have had a shot flirting. If I could remember how. Maybe there's a YouTube video for that too?

'Hurry up, girls. Back in line. Arm's length apart, remember? Just think: what would Taylor do?'

At that a few of the girls pull their shoulders back and their necks up with a kind of regal grace. I really should make up a Swifties badge for them; they could shoot their own music videos in the Hall and debate the objectification of women in the media. Or, you know, perfect her iconic red-lipped look. Personally, though, I think Taylor would be all for the debate option.

The fire engine is now gently nudging past and the thump of marching feet fills the air. I perform my own wonky pivot. Oh no. Scouts.

Hibbs didn't get so far as coming up with a special boys' group for Hazlehurst (probably because he was satisfied they'd just inherit the earth anyway. And he died at fifty-three from pneumonia, so I should give the guy some slack). So we have your common or garden Scout – woggles, campfires and really smelly feet.

But, damn it, they are pulling off an amazing march. Neat rows, uniform arm-swinging, fake smiles plastered on them like their Scout Master is holding a puppy to ransom in return for a perfect performance. Though, come to think of it, they've been without a Scout Master for a while. Not that we ever crossed paths – my Bluebells would not be seen dead sharing a camp-out with actual Scouts who might pick their nose and change their Instagram filter settings. Surely they're not going rogue? As the military-straight rows of boys near us, I'm hissing at the girls to get moving, in literally any way possible, but they are mesmerised by the chess board of boyhood stomping our way. There is going to be one epic pile-up now...

'Boys! To your left! Girls! To the right!' My Blue-bells spring to life and skip to the right-hand side of the road in an instant. They've gone from rejects for a girl band audition to some sort of terrifying fascist youth group; matching the boys for pace, getting their arms swinging too, seemingly loving it by the grins they sport.

My own mouth just falls into a slack 'Eh?!' as they pass me, slightly dizzy on the kerb by Hazlehurst Suede and Such, our local dusty shoe shop – still proud to never have stocked so much as one pair of 'training shoes'.

And at the rear, with neatly ironed khaki shorts and grey eyes that could have been made out of flint, comes what must be the new Scout Master. He nods and I nod back, changing my dribble-dropping expression to something more coherent. He's not as old as I thought a Scout Master would be. And he's a lot hotter.

'How on Earth do you…?'

But instead of slowing down or stopping or even acknowledging I've spoken, he just keeps on going. Right, left, right, left. The rude sod.

Still, the girls are moving again and no bones have been broken, not in my eyeline anyway. That's a minor success, even if I can't count it as my own.

I sneak behind the row of shops and through the local graveyard to get to the finishing point without having to lamely walk alongside the Scout Master and his sinister army of children. But I'm not going to save him any embarrassment when I find him. He can't just nick my troop and then blank me in front of half my neighbourhood. I might be a caretaker, I might own three different mops, but I have my pride.

I'm scanning rear ends around the refreshment table for sharp khaki creases and those steely eyes, but I find Abel's beaming face instead. 'Lady!'

'Hello chappy, give me a cuddle, I really need one.'

Lucy sidles up with two squashes and a frown. 'For two quid I could have bought my own bottle of squash. What are they fixing the church roof with, gold leaf?'

Abel laughs into his fat little hands. 'Leaves are green. Silly mummy.'

She sighs. 'You OK? I lost sight of you after the big girl Jenga you had going on, and then that band of Scout Stormtroopers.'

'Right? They were weird, weren't they? Eerily obedient. I don't trust any child that well behaved.'

Lucy nods as Abel takes a flying leap off a raised gravestone and lands in a bush. 'I'm going to take that as a compliment. Abel, don't annoy the dead, please.'

He tears off through the crowd. One which, frustratingly, doesn't seem to include my Scout Master target or his massive woggle.

'Have you heard who the new Scout guy is?'

'Those jungle drums haven't reached me, sorry. Why, are you going to make him a Friend of the Hall? Get his Scouts to Bob a million Jobs and fix the guttering?'

The idea is briefly tempting. 'No, I just wanted to let him know he can back off my Bluebells and not steal them for his brainless robot league.'

'Ahh, so nice to see you making new friends.'

My cheeks go hot in a flash and I'm about to say he blanked me first, when Flip and her brood appear. And they take my breath away.

Without my knowing, Flip has somehow managed to sneak off with the small length of bunting we finished sewing in the last meeting, she's strung it between two garden canes and she and her husband are carrying it between them through the crowd, lifting it above people's heads when they come to a particularly thick bunch of natterers. Their teen daughter is carrying a wind-up radio with her, blasting out jingly pop tunes. They are a mobile bunting disco. It's genius.

As they get closer, I see there are actually letters on the bunting, felt ones stuck on. 'Save Our Hall!' it reads, and behind Flip and her rugged husband, her kids are handing out fliers to anyone who'll take one. Bar Sophie, who is chewing a flier instead.

Flip takes a huge breath as she reaches me and launches into an explanation. 'Now, don't be cross but I kind of made a leap in our plan on my tod. I didn't realise the Easter parade was such a big turnout, until Martha at the grocer's filled me in. So my PR genes kicked in and I thought – I have to get our message to a captive audience! And here we are. Are you cross?' She looks up through her lashes in a way I'm sure she knows is charming and winning. I might get her to teach it to me.

'Course not! Why would you think that?'

She scuffs her red Converse on the gravel path. 'Well, it is a bit 'out there', a bit showy. Not what your gran would have done, by the sounds of it.'

My mouth opens in a knee-jerk defence of Gran, but then I realise she wasn't really showy, and thought calling attention to yourself was a bit tacky. And maybe the Hall suffered for it. I clamp my lips together again and feel a twist behind my ribs that I've just thought something disloyal about a woman who helped raise me, and who loved this place so much.

Lucy talks into the quiet I've left between us all. 'Well, maybe not, but we're moving forward, eh Connie? It's worth trying anything right now to get bodies through the door!'

Flip nods eagerly. 'Yes, exactly! And I had loads of people hum and haw excitedly about the bunting class as we made the rounds.' She jiggles her cane up and down to flap the bunting in the breeze. Her husband, who seems very well adjusted to being a quiet support act to Flip's rock-band-level energy, rolls his eyes and rubs one hand slowly across his shaved head. Flapping bunting probably isn't his number one weekend pastime of choice.

'Thank you. Thank you.' I say it and I mean it. Flip is really stepping up to help Bluebell Hall. And I'm going to do the same, but I know Gran's methods aren't all outdated and useless. She might not have been a showman, but she was a bloody good caretaker in her day.

It's time to channel Rosemarie Duncan. I'm going to need lilac slippers, a pencil and paper, and the confidence of Honey Boo Boo.

Chapter 6

OK. So maybe some things should be left in the fifties along with casual sexism and dripping on toast. And maybe some of Gran's ideas of good clean community fun should be buried deep down in the ground alongside them.

I went home the night of the parade, hoisted myself into the loft with a torch and a pack of digestives and started going back in time via all of Gran's old log books and the events she listed within. I was like Marty McFly without the orange gilet. I don't know if the air was a bit thin up there or if I ingested some long forgotten asbestos, but I came out two hours later utterly convinced that Gran had left me a message to work this Hall puzzle out. And I set about planning a few things for a week's time with the zeal of a new cult member. Because I've got just twenty days left to wrack up visitor numbers or get us an extension. I need a miracle. A miracle a lot of people would find interesting enough to come and hang out with us to see.

Just five days later and I'm no longer utterly convinced. I am utterly bricking it. And I want out of my own cult.

I should have listened to the weight in my stomach when I came to hire a floor polisher for the first of my new ventures. The price would have emptied my petty cash box, so I whacked it on my own credit card. Details, details. I'd sort it out later, I told myself. Interest charges, schminterest charges.

Using the damn thing was a bit like trying to catch a live fish from a river with hands dipped in Vaseline – it slipped and pulled away from me as it swept over the parquet floor. Turns out I hadn't really listened to the hire guy when he explained how much beeswax to use. But my cruise-ship-themed day of Hall high jinks needed a smooth floor for shuffleboard! I was going to pull in the families for this PG game instead of my usual Sunday Funday, then encourage them to stay on for buns and squash, followed by a fashion show to encourage the adults to see that the Hall wasn't just for kids' larks. That was my plan.

As I've got ten minutes before the fashion show starts, I remember that Baldrick always thought he had great plans too. And he was a flaming idiot.

The shuffleboard was not a hit. Though Steve had brought his teacher skills with the sugar paper to the Hall to help me give it an ocean liner feel – huge white clouds and blue waves and little seagulls dotted about the walls – no one really noticed. The shuffle-board pieces were picked up and examined by the little ones. And then the Carter boys realised they made pretty good impromptu ninja throwing stars and before you could say 'claims direct' they were chucking them at each other with wild abandon.

I was holding a pack of Utterly Butterly to Rod Carter's ear (the nearest thing I had on site to a bag of frozen peas) as he wept and told me he was going to kill Dan, then Preston, in that order, when I felt a wooden disc hit me squarely on the shoulder.

'Sorry!' yelped Preston. 'I was aiming for him!'

Shuffleboard got shut down.

Luckily the buns couldn't fail to be a hit, baked for me by Crusty's in a job lot, and the sticky white icing soothed away any thoughts of fratricide and kept the other bunch of kids calm too, while we waited for the parents to turn up.

Instead of bolting with their offspring, as they usually did, I got them to loiter, buns and squash in hand. And Susannah had even done a charming wander of our neighbouring roads the day before, telling people that we were having a fashion show with local models and great bargains, putting leaf-lets through doors. She'd offered to find the clothes company for me, one who'd happily bring stock in the hope of making some sales. I assumed it was one of those companies that came to her retirement home but I wasn't asking for high fashion – I'd only given her a week's notice so I was chuffed to bits with whatever. And Susannah had come up trumps in her usual calm, elegant way. She had found models, sorted the running order. She was my secret weapon.

But now my secret weapon has found herself in the middle of a very obvious war: the Carter boys, now hopped up on sugar, have snuck into the kitchen in search of more buns but found the rails of clothes to be modelled instead and have decided a game of 'jungles' is more fun, dashing in between skirts and lounge pants, leaving smears of icing on sleeves and hemlines and gussets.

Susannah is now sweating furiously as she wags her finger between the tearaways. It's just minutes before the models are due to get dressed and we have their sugary customising to deal with.

'You MUST respect the garments!' she says in a shrill tone I've never heard before.

Both boys giggle. I think they are assuming garments must be some private body part.

'Oh, get out of my sight. And don't you dare touch that cashmere as you exit!'

With two whoops, they sprint for the door.

'It's OK, Susannah,' I rub her shoulder, 'we'll sort it. And it's not the end of the world. I'm sure no one will notice.'

She turns her piercing gaze on me now and I involuntarily flinch. 'It matters to me. It matters that we put on a good show. I'm not an amateur, young lady!' She turns on her heel and dashes off in the direction of the loos and the models undressing there.

I have never seen Susannah so worked up. Not even when she and Gran fell out over a gravy recipe or when one of the Bluebells offered to help her carry her shopping across the road, when at the time she was sixty-seven.

The models are waiting in our makeshift 'wings' (the medical curtain from the school's first aid room) while Susannah talks to our assembled crowd. Our models are a mixture of locals: some of her retirement home neighbours with good hip bones, a few local shop owners and school mums, all looking pale as if they really regretted being sweet-talked by a seemingly innocent OAP.

I turn away from their nervous grimaces – the feeling is catching and my own hands feel shaky now as all eyes are focused on our walkway – and tune back into Susannah's introduction.

'... pieces that are wearable, affordable and ethically sourced. We have some beautiful linen separates, just right for the coming summer season. And my personal favourite – a charcoal grey wrap that would transition so well from chilly summer nights to a crisp autumn afternoon.'

Good, this pitch is good. I had no idea she'd put so much work into this. And when I take a second to absorb the outfits of the tremulous line behind me, I realise it's all really tasteful, subtle and… chic. This is no Jules Vert sale rail. I'd definitely wear this stuff, if I had a christening to go to, or a lovely wedding. And if I had some money.

I'm so glad now that we borrowed two spotlights from Dave the local DJ, and they are angled to hit the strips of the parquet floor that I polished especially hard for the games today. Little tea lights are lined up along the edge to mark it out (the kind that are actually battery powered, with a flickering LED in the middle) and as Susannah finishes her speech with 'Enjoy and happy shopping!' the first model, Joyce from the drycleaner's, shuffles past me to take the first walk. Two others follow suit, so there's a minimal gap between them.

Susannah comes to stand next to me and I clock that Joyce doesn't have shoes on, just her tights under a swishy navy midi skirt and Breton top. Susannah must notice my frown and whispers 'The shoes were all different colours and styles, bit unsightly for a cohesive collection, so I said to go in stockinged feet.'

I nod as if I get it. Susannah folds her arms and lets out a sigh. I think now the show is starting she can finally relax.

Sadly the same can't be said for Joyce. She is slipping and sliding and desperately trying to find her balance as she slithers about on my super shiny parquet flooring.

Oh no no no.

'No no no!' Susannah gasps.

The models behind are now joining her in their wonky ice-skating impression, pushing their feet forwards rather than taking actual steps and clinging onto each other for support. It's hardly Milan Fashion Week. It's more like a WrestleMania World Championship. Joyce nearly takes out the OAP behind her as she attempts a turn at the end, her arms flailing wildly.

Susannah drops her voice to a hiss and turns to the rest of the wide-eyed models, shrinking back towards the doors. 'Just turn on the spot, as much as you can. Don't look like we didn't plan it. Professionalism!'

I don't think this is the moment to point out that their actual professions are charity shop volunteer, bank clerk and nail technician, and that they are not actually obliged to risk breaking a leg in the name of Sunday night fashion.

Susannah's not really giving them much of an opportunity to object as she manhandles them through pastel fine knits and khaki linens, towards the Slip 'N' Slide.

I find myself calculating how far I could make the one splint kit in my first aid box go.

'Maybe we should stop thi—'

'No!'

Susannah's hands are clenched by her side. She whispers, in a kind of creepy way, 'The show must go on.'

The show did go on. It resembled a *Dancing on Ice* bloopers show, but it went on, until the last model skidded off the parquet and back behind the wings, glad to have both limbs intact under her denim play-suit.

Susannah glared at anyone giggling from the crowd and the Carter brothers wisely stayed far far away. I'm now making her a cup of tea as the saleswoman from the clothing line packs up her stock. There were a few sales, and she seemed happy with the level that came in, but Susannah had bristled that most of the audience just trooped out at the end without flashing the cash.

'Loads of sign-ins!' I chirrup, as I pass her a mug of builder's tea. 'About 60, which is ace.'

I've never really seen a retired woman harrumph. It's quite a thing. She scowls through her sips.

'It was a triumph, Susannah, really. I'm delighted. Bar the shuffleboard missiles earlier. And the ice rink. Sorry about that. Won't happen again!' As I say more and more and she keeps silent, my pitch is getting squeakier and squeakier, my shoulders scrunching up under my ears.

'In my day, I would have been fired for something like that. Such a shower of… You know what.' Her eyes flick to Gran's name on the board of caretakers, as if she's still watching our language from where she is now.

'Fired?'

'I worked in fashion. I studied at St Martin's. I was in charge of the London branch of De Rigueur fashions. In my day. Many moons ago.' She lets out a long breath, and suddenly catches my eye, the steeliness behind her gaze falling away. 'I ran shows on three hours' sleep, perfectly. Without fault. And now,' she flops down onto a stacking chair, 'now I'm an old lady who can't do anything.'

I grab her hands and gently yank her back into standing in front of me. 'Susannah! You are my rock. You are SO capable. You pulled off this scheme so quickly and so... awesomely. I had no idea you worked in fashion. When?'

She rolls her eyes. 'The days of big hair and big flares, darling. Late seventies – the glory days. But then I had my boys and that was that. You had to just give up and stay at home in those days. Career over. And not that I regret my children, not at all, but...'

'But you loved your job?'

'I did,' Susannah whispers, like it's a dirty secret. 'I really did. Gosh, I've been a silly old bird, haven't I? Treating Bluebell Hall like it's the House of Chanel!'

I squeeze her around the shoulders. 'I'd say it's currently most like a salvage yard, to be honest. And you never have to apologise about being passionate about what you do. That's perfectly normal.'

Susannah brushes imaginary crumbs off her linen skirt and pulls her shoulders up into her usual elegant poise. 'Normal to your generation, my dear. That's why I think you're so lucky, you girls: all of these paths laid out in front of you, so many exciting options waiting to be explored. Connie, you could do anything you choose.'

I pick up my tea and wrap my hands tightly around the mug, letting my fingers absorb the slightly too-hot sensation. 'Well, I do this.'

'But you didn't choose it, Connie. It's not your career. You don't see yourself here forever, do you?' Susannah blinks rapidly, her grey lashes mascara'd for tonight's event.

'Well… I've never really thought about it.' A flick book starts up in my head, one page quickly changing to the next. I'm having my 30th at the Hall, I'm sweeping up leaves outside with strands of grey in my hair, I'm going home to Mum with a small fish supper to share in a baggy pink cardigan, I'm shouting at the Bluebells for being too noisy while my hearing aid whines with feedback…

I suppose I haven't imagined myself here, doing this forever, but it's been three years of care taking already and that's gone in a few flicks of the book, with nothing much changing at all.

But as long as my roots are here, Hazlehurst is my home. With Gran gone, Mum needs me in the background. Just in case she has any low points again, any dark days where a cup of tea and a distracting natter can be crucial. And I love being around to see Abel grow up. Most days, that more than makes up for any hot shot career I might be missing out on. Besides, when I did try to 'make it big' back in

Manchester all I succeeded in doing was falling flat on my big fat face. Hazlehurst is my future now. So I need to make the best of it, and I need to hold on to the Hall.

'Um, sorry?' Sally from the fashion company sticks her head into the kitchen. 'I think you should see this. There's a problem in the bathroom. And, um… It's leaking into the hall.'

Chapter 7

Ankle deep in toilet water, Bluebell Hall didn't feel like any kind of rosy future. Clearly our toilets had given up on seeing anything more than a few school-girls a week and a bigish group of adults was just much too much for the cranky old Victorian plumbing. One of the toilets overflowed and despite plungering like crazy, I couldn't stop the water coming, so I had to switch it off at the mains. And start swishing the stinky flood out of the front door with my mop. Which is what I've been up to for the last three hours. I ordered Susannah home – spry as she is, I couldn't risk my lieutenant slipping in that mess – and it's now getting pretty dark, it took me so long to make any sort of difference to the gigantic puddle. It all feels a bit Biblical so I've been belting out 'Swing low, sweet chariot' to motivate myself through it. But when my voice gives out and my feet are too soggy to take it anymore, I decide to call it quits. There's just one more job to do before I can head home to a towel and a tea – take the black bags full of sodden paper towels out to the big bins. I do not want to find out what they'd smell like if I leave them inside for the next time the heating is switched on. Gross.

But the blummin' things are heavy – just lugging one across the gravel makes my shoulders and neck throb dangerously. So I resort to dragging the next one, and consequently split the black plastic right open, halfway to the wheelie bin. The security lights from the Hall don't quite reach that far, so I'm scooping up stinking wodges of swampy kitchen roll in the near-dark. A dream situation, all round.

The expletives rolling off my tongue would make any sailor say, 'Steady on, love,' but I'm just so tired and so filthy and so fed up. I want this to be someone else's problem, just for a minute. I don't want to be facing this on my own.

But suddenly I've lost the little light I did have and nearly scream when a tall shadow looms over me. 'Are you OK, Connie?'

I go straight for my keys in my pocket, ready to fight off any bad guys with two Chubbs and a handful of foul tissue from the ground. I could do that. I'm resourceful.

But when I clock that this man clearly knows me, my shoulders unhunch and my internal cavewoman steps back from fight duties and slopes off to tend to her fire again. In the inky night, all I can see is the glint from a silver pair of glasses and the reflective strips on the guy's fancy running beanie. Could be any of the Bluebell dads and not wanting to cause offence – and just wanting this godforsaken night to be over – I bluster on. 'Oh hey! Sorry about that, it's gone a bit Pete Tong here.'

'Can I help?' Before I can answer, the Bluebell Dad is bending down and scooping the mess up, no doubt ruining whatever clothes he's got on in this murky evening. As he straightens up, I smell something very welcome indeed – a clean, sharp lemony aftershave. It makes the hairs on my arms stand up. Must be one of the London commuting dads that I rarely see. All the more reason not to have impure thoughts about his designer fragrance. Plus, I expect a Febreze plug-in would smell like heaven to me right now.

In a jiff he's taken everything to the bins, including the two last bags that were by the front door. Rubbing his hands on his backside to clean them off, the chap then nods and says 'Goodnight, then,' sprinting off and disappearing almost as quickly as he came. My bin-bag-busting hero in Nike. Might just double check with Susannah that the local gossip mill hasn't reported any newly divorced dads in the village. Just in case.

–

At last I got home, sweet smelling home, to the giant piles of fabrics, freshly laundered and taking up my precious slumping space on the sofa. A big Post-it on top read: Iron this! Mum x

The next morning, inspecting some fresh burns on my forearms but also some pleasing stacks of colour-sorted material, the image of Hazlehurst locals shuffling like mad to stay afloat is still niggling at me, still causing an ache in the back of my head. It didn't work. Looking back through the old books for ideas had been silly, and sort of lazy. Some things are meant to be recycled – like these old shirts and tablecloths we'll soon be snipping into bunting – and some things just aren't. Like shuffleboard. I put on my trainers, lean the ladder against the loft hatch door, and put Gran's old log books back into storage. I'd always keep them there as treasured mementos, but I was retiring them from the role of How To manuals. As I went back downstairs and passed Gran's photo, I said in just above a whisper, 'Trust me, old girl. Just trust me. We're going to do this. But my way.'

Flip has been inviting more and more people to what is now a gigantic WhatsApp group called Blue-bell Bunting Bonanza – our session this Friday is going to be mammoth by all accounts. We've got WI members raring to go, A-level students sharpening their pinking shears, and more and more people popping up by the day to say they got a flier and they'd love to have a go. I'm going to have to hit Costco for a serious biscuit supply at this rate. So while our 'sucking up to the Village Committee' plan gallops ahead towards mountains of glorious bunting, I need to keep my more sneaky tack pushing on too – seeing if there's any way to extend our deadline for submitting our records, even if there's some kind of emergency fund that could help us spruce up the Hall and make it oh-so-shiny and impossible to resist.

And for this sneakiness, I need Dom's help with contracts and fine print. Seeing as the Hall still has a rather unpleasant toilet whiff about it and my living room looks like a John Lewis haberdashery sale, he's very kindly invited me round to his. Mum's pretty bright recently, so I don't feel too bad about leaving her to Fish Finger Mondays on her own. She did say she might go and see a mate if the mood struck, so here's hoping.

Dom opens the door, dressed halfway between businessman and househusband – in a navy blue suit, still with his jacket on, but with a Leicester City cooking apron on top and a tea towel slung over one shoulder. There are a few beads of sweat on his forehead. 'Sorry! Got caught up... wanted to make a spag bol from scratch but then we were late in and I couldn't find the passatta and Polly… Well,' he laughs with a weary shrug thrown in, 'Polly is Polly.'

I can hear Coldplay singing down at me from the floor above. 'Oooh, spag bol!' I make a big fuss of licking my lips. But the truth is, I can't remember when the last time was Mum or I made something from scratch so a big plate of spaghetti and a good sauce sounds blummin' amazing. I follow him into the kitchen, where pans are rattling from boiling within, and a streak of tomato sauce is making its way slowly and surely down one cupboard and to the floor. 'So did you get held up at work?' I point at his suit.

'No. It was parents' evening, and some things came up. That needed a lot of careful discussion.' I can tell by the way that he delicately pronounces these last two words that they must be the official school term for a really horrible chat.

'Oh dear.'

'Exactly. And Polly just point blank refused to go into the art teacher's room. Which I can't for the life of me understand as that's usually her best subject. She's so creative. She's always talking about being a children's book illustrator.' Though his eyes are tired and lined, there's an energy that shines out when he talks about his daughter, even if sometimes it's a nervous one.

'And she wouldn't tell you why?'

His eye rolls tells me everything I need to know. I get the feeling a conversation shift is in order. So I tap the big wedge of papers I have clamped under my left arm.

'Well, I think I found just about everything relevant to the Hall tenancy in here, and I've read it all and made some notes. So if I can ask you to decode the odd bit or just have your best stab, after we've tucked in…'

'Sounds like a plan. Just pop them on the top of the piano for now. Grub's up.'

I help Dom carry through a plate and a bowl of salad, as he yells up the stairs, 'Pol! Connie is here and dinner's ready!'

There's a light clatter of feet and Polly appears, still in her uniform, her olive skin impossibly clear but her eyes framed by grey bags. I want to ask if no one in this family has joggers to change into when they get home – it's like they're both more comfortable in the uniforms from their 'other' lives, away from the house. Work and school. Home is just somewhere to begrudgingly pass the hours before you can leave again. I'm feeling self-consciously casual in my jeans and old uni sweater, my dark bob wavy and messy as yet another chance for a blow dry is ignored in favour of a quick game of Candy Crush. Maybe to fit in with their uniform stylings I should have gone for some caretaking dungarees?

She gives me a genuine smile and plops down on a chair next to where I'm sitting. 'How are things, Polly?'

'Yeah, you know.' She twirls a fork round in her pasta. I think those two words are meant to express something, but I'm fifteen years too old to understand what.

'Right. Well, we're all set for the next bunting meeting. Loads of great fabrics, amazing colours, all the sewing machines oiled up and in working order. Just need to make sure our art director is there to have it all come together beautifully.' I nod in her direction.

She winces a little. 'Oh, yeah. But someone else could do it, I don't know… What if I mess it up?'

My Bluebells duties have taught me that just about every girl has a well of self doubt, and without it being boarded up properly, confidence can just slip away into its dark depths. Dom hasn't said anything, he's pushing garlic bread around with a twitchy hand. So I'm going to nail a big wooden cover over this.

'You'll be great. I mean,' I look around for inspiration and see her fingers drumming on the pine table, 'take your nails for example. I would never have thought a turquoise like that could look so good next to a lemon yellow, but you've chosen two different colours and mixed and matched them up a treat. That's exactly what I need you to do on Friday. And you're already smashing it!'

Polly sits back in her chair, holding her hands up in front of her as if she'd forgotten they were there. 'You think? Um. OK. Cool. I'll be there.'

'Well, it'll be nice to know where you are for that night at least.' Dom shoves the last edge of his bread into his mouth.

Polly is hiding her hands in the armpits of her school cardigan now, glowering madly at him.

We've avoided the Well of No Confidence and tumbled straight into the Quicksands of a Row. It suddenly hits me why Mum and I don't have so many full-on family dinners… And I don't really want to get sucked into this one, so I clap my hands and plunge into a new subject. Maria Von Trapp would be proud.

'So your dad says you're into art? I always loved art. And the design side of things too, I did a Textiles course at school. Kind of the cheat's way into arty stuff if you can't draw, like me.'

Polly rolls her eyes and it's not just her Mediterranean complexion she's got from her dad – they have the same weary eye roll down to a T. 'I used to like it. Whatevs.'

I feign innocence. 'But not any more?'

A sudden burst of anger makes Polly sit bolt upright and talk slightly too loudly. 'Stupid Miss Ingram and her stupid projects. They're just bullshit!'

'Polly!' Dom roars. 'Language! And don't speak disrespectfully of your teachers.'

'If you knew what she was asking—'

'I don't care. You don't talk like that in front of me, or guests. Or anyone.'

'But she's making us do... It's a...' Polly scrunches up her eyes and bolts for the door.

–

Dom and I finished the rest of our meal quickly and awkwardly got down to the nitty gritty of the Hall paperwork. I was dying to ask him if he wanted me to wait while he went after Polly, but I knew that was well over the line and not something I would do with a Bluebell family I'd known for years, let alone brand new friends. And though I spend a lot of time with pre-teens and their dilemmas, they are mostly about hair styles and I've never been a full-time parent, let alone a single one.

He pointed out where there was a clause about challenging any decision of the estate by writing to its board directly, and gave me some good tips on how to write it very formally but clearly, CCing in my local councillor and MP, to really show I meant business. I took feverish notes on my phone and mentally began to compose sentences containing words like 'forthwith', 'inconceivable' and 'notwithstanding'. After an hour I think we've both taken all the tiny copperplate script we can take and I thank Dom for his excellent spag and his even better contract cooking. I feel full of cheese but also of promise: we might wriggle our way out of a loophole on this one.

He lets me out into the crisp spring evening with a promise to be at Friday's meeting with bells on.

As I'm walking down his garden path, I hear a light crunching of gravel. And instantly the reconstruction of my murder in *Crimewatch* flashes through my mind. Will they find an extra with exactly my kind of fringe?

But I can see the toes of a pair of smallish acid pink trainers in the gloom, a little way down the side of the house. So unless serial killers are wearing size four Sketchers these days, I think it's safe to approach.

'Polly?'

'Oh hey. I'm not being weird. I just like to sit here, sometimes. For a bit of headspace.' She swinging her legs back and forth, sitting on a weather-beaten bench that's been parked down the side passage.

'Sure. I get it. Can I?'

She shrugs.

'So, you never quite said what exactly was such a pain about that art teacher. What has she done?'

Polly lets out a big fat sigh. 'Ugh. I thought she was OK. We did still life, and Pop Art, and mosaics and junk. But now… Look, I didn't mean to be a nut job earlier. I'm not a diva. It's just, some things get me,' her hands turn circles in the air, 'mixed up.'

'Well, who isn't mixed up around here?'

She laughs a little bit. 'It's a family tree project. Miss Ingram wants us to do a family tree in an original way. And it's not fair. Because what if, what if, you don't have that much family to use? I mean our family is a stump. Just two of us. It's, like, I could just write our names down and put one line in between. That's it.' She picks at a painted-yellow thumbnail.

I choose my words very carefully, like trying to avoid the strawberry creams in a box of Quality Street, if the strawberry creams also contained explosives. 'You can put family that aren't actually still with you, in a family tree. Go back another generation, too. Add some branches and leaves to that stump. And it's nice to reflect everyone in your family, because even if they aren't here they made your family what it is.'

A pair of dark brown brows meet over her eyes. 'But how are you supposed to do it all 'uniquely'? Like, a tree is a tree?'

I think about all the generations of people filtering down into this one girl. Completely unique in herself, the way genes have combined and behaviours have been learned. Little pieces of the family that have gone before still in her bones. But one big thing missing. One big thing that keeps tripping her up, every day, even in her favourite class.

'I might just have an idea. Got a sketch book in there? And do you think your dad would let you come over to mine one day this week?'

–

As I walk slowly home, I think about the bits of Gran and Mum in me. The things I am so glad to carry with me, and the things that make me sad that I miss Gran and that this situation maybe isn't the bed of roses it could be. And if I'm going to dish out ideas to Polly about embracing what has been and gone but putting our own creative spin on it, I'd better be willing to eat a big plate of that advice myself. I have to ask myself: if we can save the Hall, if we can pull off this trick worthy of *Ocean's 14*, do I actually want to be the caretaker forever? Am I in it for a forty-year stint, like Gran? I know that I want to put my own spin on things here now, rather than just going through the motions, but what about when my new ideas become the norm?

There's so much of Gran in me, and in my nature, but that doesn't necessarily mean we should have exactly the same paths in life, does it? The Hall was everything to Gran, but will it be enough for the rest of my life?

Chapter 8

'Blimey O'Reilly!'

Flip drops her gold lamé satchel on the floor with a wallop. 'This is… This is… Whoah. Connie, I bow down to you, girl. This is amazing.' She puts her arms out and spins on the spot. Her hands point to the fuchsia pink wall, then the teal wall, the sunny yellow all around the doorway and the crisp bluebell blue on the fireplace wall. The same colours that I'm still finding flecks of under my nails and in my eyebrows, funnily enough.

'You did all this?' Susannah walks in slowly behind her. I've been nervous of her response especially, but her gobsmacked lips quickly find a smile shape. 'Divine!'

'It really is!' Flips nods and clasps her hands together, like this is her living room after a *DIY SOS* reveal. 'It's like a new space entirely.'

I shove my hands in my back pockets, hoping to seem more laid back about their reactions than I am. 'That's what I was going for. I thought – if they're going to take this place away, or try to at least, why am I obsessing over keeping the original and, let's be honest, awful Victorian wallpaper? No one likes it, it doesn't make anyone feel cheery. But colours do. Bright and positive and clean. And it just so happens that one of my old school mates works at B&Q so he used his discount on some end of the line paints. His sister was a Bluebell back in the day, so he did me a solid favour.' I shrug, the movement reminding me that my shoulders and neck aren't quite recovered from the last three days' worth of rollering and edging and general lugging of huge paint cans.

After I talked with Polly, and still thinking about those nail varnish colours of hers, I suddenly had an amazingly clear vision of how the Hall should be. Not a legacy of the past, but a reflection of what our village is now and where we want it to go. It needs to be an uplifting place to capture a moment, not a mausoleum to the past. So I got busy with brushes and dust sheets. And I'm damn pleased with it. The exertion also helped silence the voice in my head, asking me what exactly my life plan would be when our 17 days are up. That voice can be gagged for now; it's hardly helping matters at hand.

I wanted to keep the reveal as a big surprise for Flip, Susannah and Luce tonight: we're having a little pre-meet before tomorrow night's Bunting Society meeting. The numbers are now up to almost twenty of us, so Flip suggested (from her past life of organising big events and groups of people) that we get together, the core of us, beforehand and have a bit of a plan. I can see she is enjoying flexing her PR knowhow and I am definitely loving having her expertise on my side. I don't have time to waste, and there's so much at stake.

'Kettle on, then. And we can crack on. I expect Luce will be here soon, commuting and all.'

From within the kitchen (not yet painted but I have my eye on a very light green that should open the dingy space up a bit) I can hear a clatter of heels and then, 'Christ on a bike!' Lucy is here.

–

We're moving through the production line of our big fete bunting: firstly how each table will be laid out, where the materials will be kept, who'll be overlooking each station. And then whether we have enough pennant templates, scissors and bias binding. Finishing with, essentially, the tea rota by the half hour.

'And then the sewn, trimmed and reversed pennants are brought over to Lucy's table, where some of our best stitchers,' Susannah pauses to wink at Flip, and they enjoy a little moment of co-sewing nerdiness, 'will sew them with the bias binding, at roughly 25 centimetres apart. And we keep going until we have 500 metres' worth. Enough for the park railings, come the fete.'

Lucy lets out a low whistle. She's scrutinising the sewing machine like it's a bomb she's been sent to safely defuse. 'That's a lot of bunting. And we want to achieve it all on Friday, right?'

I chew the inside of my lip a little. 'Yes, because we need to get it to the Committee really soon, so they can wade in on our appeal in time. We need their big cojones. Oh, um, sorry Susannah.'

When she looks blank, Flip leans in and whispers a translation in her ear.

Susannah grasps her pearls. 'Oh. Right.'

Lucy is calculating away in her head, I can tell. She's scanning the room, counting, sizing things up. 'Shall we do a test run here, for say 10 metres, and time ourselves? Then we'll know tomorrow if we're on the right track, time-wise.'

I've never known Luce to say anything that wasn't as sensible as a pac-a-mac on a British holiday, so I'm happy to follow her direction. Some people expected us to hate each other when Steve first brought her back to live in Hazlehurst but I never understood that. Firstly, she's brave – she took on the prospect of sorting him out. Secondly, she's funny – her speech at their wedding still makes me laugh when I think of it now, and thirdly, you can never have too many smart, kick-ass friends. I love her just as much as I do Steve now.

We take up our positions: me drawing and cutting triangles of fabric, Susannah sewing them, Lucy trimming and turning them the right way out, then passing them on to Flip, who sews them onto the binding.

There's something so hypnotic about crafting. I'd almost forgotten it – usually with craft activities for the little ones at the Hall or the Bluebells, I'm too busy dishing out the PVA and newspaper to really get elbow deep myself. But almost instantly I get lost in picking a handful of nice fabrics, placing my templates on them to use what I've got as wisely as possible and feeling the satisfying clunky snip of extremely sharp scissors. I can see success in what I do – I'm taking something flat, and without an obvious use, and starting it off on the path to be something lively and gorgeous. Something happy. Because show me one person who doesn't feel at least five per cent happier when they see bunting.

Luce sidles up while we have a quick tea break. There's working hard and then there's taking the correct fuel breaks. I mean, we *are* British. 'At this rate I think it will be tight, but we might just do it, with everyone working together,' she says. 'Something you might have remembered when you were having your Sistine Chapel moment.' She points up at the ceiling.

'What do you mean?'

'I mean, all you had to do was text Steve or me and say you wanted a hand. This must have taken you day and night.'

I wave her concerned look away with one flick of my wrist. 'You guys have got your life, this is mine right now.'

'Risking your neck up a ladder, totally alone, probably knackered through overwork? Wow, you should give motivational seminars on achieving your dreams!' Luce deadpans. 'Seriously, though, I get that you are really driven and passionate, and that's why we all love you. But we do love you and we're here to help you. So please let us. See how much more we're all doing as a four than we would if it was just you sweating over a Singer? And when there's twenty of us we'll really be kicking butt. You've got to let people in, hun. That's all I'm saying.' She nudges me with her shoulder and goes back to her work.

–

It's Friday night and with the newly expanded Blue-bell Society filling the newly painted Hall, there's an energy here I haven't felt since it was my tenth birthday party and Mum and Gran filled the place with purple balloons (my favourite colour), hired a mini bouncy castle and put smiley faces on all my fairy cakes.

Everyone is just about ready and assembled but we're missing two vital members: Dom and Polly. I send a quick text to Dom.

> Hey! You guys OK?

> Sorry. Ten mins late. Polly missing

My heart leaps into my chest. She's missing? Oh my god. What should we do?

But another text pings in straight after it.

> Missing bus home didn't help. will be there just as soon as she's changed.

With a long exhale, I put my phone in my back pocket and go and ready some big jugs of squash and the tea urn Flip has borrowed from the WI. Tea means bunting, this much we know.

'Room for a little one?' Steve's voice makes me leap out of my skin, as I'd been daydreaming about bunting flapping in the breeze, decorating the fete and charming everyone nearby, and them all whispering, 'Yes, it was made at the Hall. By hand! I'm going to have my grandson's christening party there, you know.'

'Jeez, Stevie, practise your ninja creeping skills much? Anyway, what are you doing here? Did Luce forget something?'

'Just her secret, ripped missile.' He kisses a bicep and pulls an Arnie pose.

'Huh?'

He knocks me on the forehead with his knuckles, just a touch too hard. 'I'm here to help, numpty. Abel's tucked up with granny, for the whole weekend might I smugly add, and seeing as my lovely lady wife can't stop talking about how great the Hall is looking and about these plans of village domination and legal battles, I thought I should get a piece of the action.'

It's probably not until I take in his words and see his big dorky smile that I realise I've been carrying my shoulders up to my hairline so far tonight. Something eases off inside enough for me to laugh. 'Well, I can't wait to see how you handle a sewing machine.'

'I was thinking of more of a support role – mopping brows, fitting thimbles, pouring tea through a funnel. Luce tells me that the way I put ties and shirts together means I should never get close to any fabric design choices. Here, let me,' he takes over the filling of the kettle and the assembling of mugs, 'you go off, do some leader-like thing. Everyone is here because of you, you know.'

I look into the busy, bustling hall full of keen local faces. There's a burble of happy chatter in the background as the tables are being set up and supplies laid out. We could do it tonight. It could really happen. And in trying to save the Hall, it's getting a much longed-for taste of its original purpose – to bring Hazlehurst together, to let villagers share memories and pastimes. Even if we come out of this session with half a metre of wonky bunting and pin-puncture fingers, in a way I'll still be happy.

Two new faces appear at the door: Dom and Polly, at last. So now it's really time to begin.

–

We sewed until our vision blurred. We snipped until the scissors went dull and our conversation went ever duller. Lengths of bias binding whizzed through the machine in front of Flip like she was Rumpelstiltskin with a barn's worth of straw at his disposal. Checks met spots and plain fabrics nestled up to chintz, colours complimented and clashed and chattered together. Polly has one brilliant eye for colour. Well, two in fact. She really got into the groove of arranging patterns as the pennants came her way and even shyly began chatting to the older teens there, from the college. Everyone dug deep and pulled out bags of energy, while Steve watered them with tea, like little sewing sunflowers.

The one thing we hadn't planned to within an inch of our sanity? How we'd store the stuff after we'd made it. And loose bunting is like summer's equivalent of a bunch of Christmas fairy lights, tangling itself into a headache-worthy mess. Thinking on my feet as the glorious team worked like a Home Ec teacher on ten espressos, I found one of the noticeboards I'd taken down in my painting blitz. And I started winding. That became my little task of the night and it allowed me to survey the troops, stop anyone getting so knackered that they almost ran a needle over their thumb (Flip) or so hungry they were unknowingly chewing off most of a BIC (Luce). Stevie proved himself an excellent support person, was nicknamed Francis Nightingale by the WI crew, and provoked a lot of giggling and ogling from the A-levellers. Gross, to my mind, but they are from a girls' school. So, slim pickings.

I was so poleaxed by exhaustion myself that by the end of the night I couldn't even face a proper tidy-up or an official metre count. It would have been great to do the bit at the end of *Comic Relief* where they whip out the totaliser at 2 a.m. and announced they've smashed their record and everyone has a happy cry. But there were a few locals who were just on the verge of a pinking shears phobia at 10.30 p.m., so I booted everyone out with a promise of a WhatsApp update first thing on Saturday morning. I would arm myself with a sausage roll from Crusty's and tackle the sorting then, I vowed.

My body clearly had other thoughts and Mum shook me awake at eleven a.m., with a bacon sarnie right under my nose. 'Come on, hardworking girl. Let's get something in your system. I think someone's been overdoing it.'

Mum sat on the bed while I wolfed down the sandwich and filled her in, mid-bite, on all the goings-on at the Bunting Society. I could have been twelve and telling her about my Gymnastic meet final. Sometimes when she had her dark days when I was little, she wouldn't make my school plays or come see me awkwardly leap over the vault and land nose-first in a crash mat. But Gran would be a worthy stand-in and Mum always made a point when she felt stronger of getting me to rattle off a full update over hot chocolate and toast. Yes, I would rather have had her there – and it made me angry when I was young – but Gran carefully explained to me that it was far from Mum's choice. It was in fact the last thing she'd want to happen, and she needed our patience more than anything.

Mum nodded and smiled throughout this update and I couldn't see bags under her eyes or that grey tinge to her skin she gets when she's been inside for weeks on end. She was feeling good.

'Don't speak with your mouth full, love. But it sounds marvellous. I think I'll come next time!' I could only smile in response, red sauce on my teeth, because we both knew what a big statement that was.

I had the world's fastest shower, probably the equivalent of a wet wipe, but I just couldn't wait to get back to Bluebell Hall and take stock of our achievements. It was like knowing your birthday presents are waiting in the kitchen and almost throwing yourself down the stairs to get there faster.

At the Hall approximately seven minutes later, I figure out my measuring strategy – I mark two spots on the parquet with chalk, three meters apart, and then I walk back and forth with the unspooled bunting between the marks so all I have to do when it's all laid out is count the lengths and times them by three. Genius. And the pacing is good for balancing out all the custard creams I ate last night.

I stop counting my laps somewhere around twenty-three and let my mind wander to the next stages of our plan. We'll present the bunting to the

Village Committee, charm them into supporting us. My letter is with the Hibbert Estate already, so I'll have to play the waiting game for a response and hopefully an extension. We have two weeks left — it is just about do-able. Just. But I still want more locals to know what we are trying to achieve, more bodies through the door. I should ask Flip for more of her PR know-how in grabbing attention, and maybe any experience Dom has with advertising through his business. I can't keep banging on about the Hall's place in history; it needs to feel relevant to the village of today. So my ideas should be just as fresh and modern. I used to know all the crazy, hip stuff when I still lived in a big city but now I'm about as edgy as a satsuma. I developed a bit of an allergy to anything too trendy after my time at *B-Side*, so it's best left to the youth. I whip out my phone and make a note in my To Do list: Ask Polly about Pinterest. What the heck is it.

I'm just dreaming about what kind of role I could make for Mum in the process — maybe Budgens would let us put some leaflets by the tills and she could chat to customers about what was going on? Maybe, if she was feeling up to all that interaction. And then the clap of the letterbox catches me out, once again.

Surely not. On a Saturday? If it's anything like the last bit of post here…

With a weird surge of anger, I leg it to the door and sprint outside before my besuited postman can escape.

'Hey!' I yell to the back of a crisp white shirt. 'Oi! Wait right there!'

He freezes. And turns on the spot, a few feet from his car and any hope of an escape.

It's the sodding Scout Master.

My rage slides into embarrassment as I remember his flinty eyes blanking me at the parade. But social awkwardness can do one, I'm not letting him get away without some sort of explanation.

I wave the letter I scooped up on my run out here. 'So can I take it you also hand deliver for the Hibbert Estate, as well as teaching the military art of marching to under 12s?'

His jaw sets and I can tell he's taking his time to think of a polite response. 'I'm currently employed as a financial consultant for the estate, yes.'

'Which means, to us common folk...'

'Which means I'm helping them assess the Hall in its current state and usage and put together a series of next steps.'

'Such as flogging it to Costa or tearing it down for a new block of flats?'

I can see by the spot of colour that begins to show above his cheekbones that I'm onto something.

I was just being dramatic, all hopped up on self-righteousness. I didn't actually want to be right! My stomach gives a weird gurgle of panic.

He clears his throat. 'I help communities. In the same way I help people who are struggling with defunct plumbing systems and bags of rotting paper towels, even when I'd rather be enjoying a nice, sweet-smelling run through the village.'

A big stinky penny drops. It was the Scout Master that night, who helped me with the bin bags. Not a hot Bluebell dad. I am so baffled by this admission that all I can do is steamroll on with my frustrations.

'Well, let me show you something about how sweet this village really is.' I grab him by the shirt sleeve and physically drag him through the front doors. He could very well stop me if he wants to – he's really rather tall and I can feel some muscles going on under my grip – but I think we're both so shocked that I'm actually doing this that before we know it we're smack bang in front of my bunting census. I remember to drop his shirt sleeve before I launch into another soapbox moment.

'This hall is part of our village life. We're not giving up easily and I will prove to you this hall is still used just as Hibbs... William Hibbert intended.' My air jabbing finger comes to rest, pointing at the team handicrafts by our feet.

His eyes narrow. 'What… Is that bunting?'

'Yes!' I realise I'm not doing myself any favours in the way I'm blurting things out, ten to the dozen, and the sudden wave of nervous sweat is not really detracting from my 'crazy lady' demeanour right now. 'Made by many, many Hazlehurst hands. And more will come. You'll see!' Oh, I've actually veered into Scooby-Doo villain territory now.

'Right.' He puts his hands into his annoyingly stylish suit pockets. 'And how will that make a difference? Some bunting on the floor?'

With my resounding 'Pfft!' of annoyance, I manage to get some spit on his shirt collar. Excellent. The cherry on top of the bat shit cake. 'That's for you to find out, Mr…'

'Alex. Alex Granger, Miss Duncan.'

Christ, he knows just who I am. Putting it down to an 'unstable temp' is not going to help me gloss this over when I have to come face to face with the Estate Board. Brilliant.

So I steam on. The perfect antidote to chatting rubbish is of course to lay some more rubbish quickly on top. And maybe this will all turn out to be a bad custard-cream-related dream. 'And it's not on the floor, not like that. I'm measuring it. Because we've made loads. As a community team.'

Alex nods, infuriatingly calm in the face of my verbal diarrhoea. 'You should have made the markers bigger.'

'What?'

'If you're measuring between these two markers, and you obviously have a lot to measure by the looks of it, you should have spaced them further apart. It would have been more efficient.'

Mansplaining. That's exactly the kind of kerosene my white hot anger needs right now. He might as well have called me sweet pea and told me to put the kettle on.

I clench and unclench my fists. I did not polish this floor just to stain it with Scout Master blood. I will be calm.

I let out one breath very slowly through my teeth. 'Right. And you just make a habit of working on a Saturday in a full fancy suit, do you?' Why did I say fancy!? 'Your social calendar must be bursting at the Saville Row seams.'

His eyes suddenly avoid mine, inspecting his highly polished shoes instead. That was possibly too much, but I can't think straight for the steam coming out of my ears.

After clearing his throat, Alex says calmly, 'I always dress appropriately for work matters,' his eyes flick to my Stone Roses t-shirt, 'and I thought you'd want to receive this response as soon as possible.'

'Response?'

He nods and points to the letter in my sweaty grasp. 'We received your request for an extension. But we politely decline – within our rights,' he hastily adds, as if that's going to calm me down.

I'm starting to think I could live with blood stains. 'You must have given it all of five seconds' consideration, then,' I mutter.

'Honestly, it was the opposite.'

I fold my arms. 'Well, thanks. So much. For the personal touch.'

His shoes click clack on the parquet as he leaves. 'Nice paint job,' echoes back from the front door. But with the echo, I can't tell if he's being sarcastic.

Chapter 9

Even in the tranquil setting of Crusty's, with teacups gently chinking in the background and a bready steam buffeting the shop window, I am still roaring with rage inside my head. There are only three little tables in the front of the bakery, I think more for a cosy effect than to house lots of customers, but we've pulled them all together for an emergency Bunting Society summit. Gran's sewing basket is in the middle of the table, as inspiration, with a length of our new bunting tying the lid down. Still, a few odds and ends are threatening to burst out.

Pausing only to lick scone crumbs from my lips, I've painted the full picture of my run-in with Alex. Who I call The Suit, in my best withering voice.

'And then he just ran away! With some nasty little comment about my painting skills.'

Susannah gasps.

'I mean, it sounded nasty. What he said. The way he said it was unpleasant. I'm pretty sure. But the long and short of it is: no extension, guys. Just fifteen days until we have to submit our records to save Bluebell Hall — and although we've been pulling out the stops to get those numbers up, we're still a way off. We need to pull the stops out of the stops now. We need to be utterly stop-less. No idea is too mad for me. I'll try anything!' I cram another half of scone into my mouth, realising too late it was Lucy's. She kicks me under the table.

'We need more people to know just how serious the situation is. We need our message out there, with the media. Local for starters.' Flip waves her hand at the high street through the shop window, her royal blue nails flashing in the spring sunlight.

'So, in your expert opinion, Flip, how do we do that? How do we get the media to sit up and take notice?'

She drums her fingers against her chin, dislodging a few bun crumbs at the same time. 'Pictures speak a thousand words. It's a cliche but for a reason. If you can give them an eye-catching photo op that will make a blinding first page, then the hard work is all done for them. Bish bash bosh.'

Luce looks mournfully at her empty plate. 'Shame the damp patches at Bluebell Hall aren't more attractive. Maybe one has the image of Ant and Dec in it, and we could sell tickets to the miracle?'

I pat her hand. 'Let's keep praying for that to happen. But in the meantime, I think we probably need a photo op to happen away from the Hall for now, somewhere else in the village that reflects the heart of the community.'

Susannah points her teaspoon in my direction. 'The bunting all strung up at the fete would be stunning, and absolutely the heart of the village.'

'But too late – that's only a few days before the deadline and we need wheels in motion before then.' Flip turns out her bottom lip. 'We need something that gets people out of their seats, a water cooler moment. And soon.'

A flashback comes to me: temping in Manchester and Svetlana from accounts pulling me to the window because there was a flash mob dancing about in the street below. We'd abandoned our spreadsheets and joined the crowd gawping and clapping to the beat. That had been about toilet cleaner, it turned out (playing 'Flash' by Queen should have been our first clue) but the fact is, it's stuck in my mind all this time. Effective.

Shame that my track record of organising public dance routines is not exactly flawless. And how would you dance about bunting? That feels a bit too bonkers, even for us. No, the bunting has to show itself off. It has to be the star of the show.

'Guys, I might have an idea. It could work, or it could be OTT, that's the thing.'

Flip beams. 'In PR, OTT is our blood type. Go Las Vegas OTT. Go Elton at Vegas OTT. With bells on, feather boas if you can.'

'Well, that's a relief because that's pretty much what I'm thinking. I will need a bit of time to flesh it out, then I'll spill.'

She fist bumps me. 'Brill! I'll be on email tonight when the kids are in bed.'

'Kids should be one of our angles, you know,' Susannah muses. 'To pull the local heartstrings. I doubt most of the parents at the school know that if the Hall goes, so do the Bluebells and an important social and educational activity for their girls.' She takes a decisive gulp of her Earl Grey.

I'm not sure spending ninety minutes with me a week can be described as socially or educationally stimulating, but I do let the girls debate their own cultural issues (Beyoncé: better with or without Jay Z?) and answer their questions about the world truthfully and openly (But why are boys SO awful?).

Lucy taps her fingers against her glass. 'We have our redheaded Adonis in the system.'

I shake my head, confused.

'Steve!'

'Oh god, Luce, please.'

'Horses for courses. But maybe there's a way we could get some bunting into the school. If Steve could use it for a class project, that would be a way of getting parents more informed.' She grabs Gran's sewing bits with both hands in a snap move. 'Yes! *Fantastic Mr Fox*!' She pulls out a strip of leftover fake fur. 'The kids could make Fox bunting for the play! Steve would love it. The fur could be little dangling tails.'

I tick off on my fingers. 'So, media. Parents. Who else?'

'I'm going to butter up Malcolm at the library. As a fellow threatened building, he should get behind us more. Maybe a history night there next week, talking through the village's long record of charitable patrons, and we could end with a walk up to the Hall and examining Hibbert's memorial.'

'Brill! I am loving these ideas, guys. Just kicking myself I didn't hit on them earlier.'

'You weren't faced with closure in two weeks' time, earlier.' Flip pats my shoulder. 'There's nothing like a deadline to really spur on creativity.'

We've been jabbering back and forth since we got here, but so far Dom and Polly have kept to their Chelsea buns and not much else.

Polly lets out a tiny 'Um?'

'Yes, Pol?'

'I don't know if this is what you're after… Or if it will make that much difference…'

'All ideas are good ideas!' Flip flashes her a double thumbs up.

Polly fiddles with a length of her dark red hair. 'I've kind of used bunting in this art project, about family trees. Connie helped me, actually. And I liked… It was good for me to use the sewing and stuff to put some feelings out there. Into the world. So I wondered if it might help others too?' She's now fully pink after speaking so long with all eyes on her and if it wasn't crushingly uncool, I'd hug this gorgeous, nervous teen, right down to her marrow.

'Like an art therapy group?' Susannah asks.

'Suppose.' Polly's most likely used her quota of words for the month so we might not get more out of her. I wonder if visual aids might help.

'Did you bring it with you, your project?'

'Oh, yeah.' She scrabbles in a micro backpack stuffed with tissues and lip balms and slowly pulls out a jumble of bunting triangles. When she holds them up properly and the design unfurls down into an upside-down triangle, I can see just what a beautiful thing she's made.

It's darker triangles of denim and green cord making the top row of five pennants – and on four of them, with a plain one in the middle, she's embroidered the names of her grandparents. Then the three pennants sewn below those have her parents' names and an ampersand sewn on artfully against fabrics of floral prints and a golden yellow velvet. And the bottom, a single triangle is a full-bodied purple with Polly Dexter sewn onto it in an old style tattoo font. Her choices of materials and lettering reflect the generations of people she is capturing in her very unique family tree. If Miss Ingram doesn't give her an A and five gold stars, I'll be having words.

'You can use things that mean something. To, like, preserve them forever but in a way that makes you feel OK about it. So this is...'

Her finger wobbles at the floral material and her voice peters out.

'Your mum's bedspread.' Dom finishes for her. 'I wondered where that had gone. And her velvet jacket for best. Well.' He thickly swallows a mouthful of bun and washes it down with tea.

There is a long silence. Polly's eyes are glued to Dom like a car accident – she's scared but she's can't help wanting to see how he's going to react.

React, Dom, react! You daft man! I'm screaming at him in my head. Show this girl she's brave and talented, even if it's hard!

I see Lucy's hands grip the arms of her seat. She must be bursting to yell the same.

'Well,' he rubs a hand over his stubble, 'well, funny kind of family tree, eh?' His light laugh, maybe an attempt to be jovial, lands very heavily. Polly shuts her eyes, hard, for a beat.

'Thanks.' She stuffs the artwork back in her bag in brutal shoves.

'I, for one, love your piece. And I am all for an art therapy group,' Susannah finally says, breaking the awkward tension. 'I think it would help so many of my neighbours, who have lost loved ones. Or are losing their memories. We just won't tell the care workers exactly where the class is. It won't hurt this one time to flaunt a little health and safety.'

'Susannah, you minx!' I laugh, just as Flip gives a little cackle, and the tension is gone. 'Is this how you do it?' Susannah holds up her knuckles and I realise she's waiting for a fist bump.

'Sounds like we've all got lots to do. Pol, I love the art therapy idea. It's a total winner and your family tree will be the perfect example of sewing something that has real meaning. You know, when I was reading up on craft blogs I came across this study that says using your fingers for fine sewing work actually helps maintain a healthy, working brain? So you would be doing a world of good for the village, Polly. We'll get some fliers going, pick a date for the first class very soon. OK? Let's finish our scones, and get cracking. You know where I'll be if you need me!'

–

Kidnapping is a strong word. I mean, it's a proper crime, I get that, but sometimes a bit of light kidnapping for a good cause isn't so bad. That's what I'll tell my priest. Or possibly my barrister.

It was easy enough to crash the Village Committee meeting – they are open to locals, so we can all vote on the theme of this year's Christmas lights and the May Day Queen election and such. What was trickier was politely cornering the chairman Brian Hicks and persuading him there was some appalling local graffiti that needed his attention, and to follow me straight away.

'At the Hall?' he'd spluttered. 'That's appalling! I mean, it's not really my remit, but it says 'Hazlehurst Sucks' you say? It must be those Latimer scoundrels. Just because they had their village of the year 2009 rosette overturned by an anonymous source exposing their use of fake flowers!' He pulled at his collar with one finger. Brian, I thought, you're no stranger to an underhand tactic yourself.

I frog-marched him towards the Hall from the church, wringing my hands at what a tragedy it was, and whatever was I to do. If this caretaking lark did fall through, I could always take a run at *Hollyoaks*.

But Brian isn't met by a wall of acid green scrawl and neighbourhood hate speech. When he pokes his red face into the Hall he sees a glorious web of freshly made bunting, strung back and forth from the rafters. Greens and yellows, soft purples and punchy reds. The crisp zigzag of the sheared fabric looks neat and precise, the playful, artful use of patterns and tones brings in energy and fun on top. If I didn't know better I would have said it was a beautiful Liberty's display or the launch of a new yacht. But I do know better: it's Bluebell Hall in a whole new light.

'Good gracious!'

'Mr Hicks, do forgive my little pantomime there, but on behalf of the Bluebell Bunting Society, may I gift to your committee almost 550 metres of bespoke bunting for the May Day fete.' At the last minute I pull myself back from a full on curtesy.

He lets out a wheeze of a breath. I'm not sure if he's dead impressed or just nearly dead from the speed walking here. 'Really? Is that a real thing, then? A bunting society.'

'It is now!' I breeze on. 'Formed out of necessity – because Bluebell Hall is under threat from corporate development. I'm not sure what your stance is on big businesses coming into the village, erasing our history, Mr Hicks?'

'Oof, yes, no. Awful. Worse than graffiti!'

'Well, let me fill you in on the full story. Perhaps over a cup of tea and custard cream?'

–

After my success at swamping the Committee chairman with coordinated fabrics and impassioned pleas for help, I slept like a baby. A big, drooling baby who lurches awake when the alarm goes off at six a.m. Yes, I could do with a lot more sleep. But Flip and I are on a dawn mission.

I pull on jeans and my Stone Roses t-shirt, the first thing to hand but sadly also the first thing on top of some mouldy smelling washing, run a hand through my lanky bob and bolt. Luckily no one will see but Flip. Secrecy is key.

When I reach the top of the high street after a stomach-churning jog, I take one long gulp of air. Not just because of the strain of the jog on my out-of-shape body, but because the village I knew is unrecognisable for the first time in my life.

The shops here have sustained me through all the funny little stages of my development – wasting pocket money on notepads and stickers in the stationer's as a primary school kid, moving on to nail varnishes in Mr Singh's pharmacy when hormones finally hit. The pond tucked behind the shops, where we'd go as fifteen-year-olds with our first boyfriends, to hold hands and talk about nothing and do nothing, then endlessly analyse the nothing with our mates later. The ancient church with its toffee-box-perfect arch of roses is where I was christened and where my mum hopes (and hopes and hopes) I'll get married one day. I'll give it to her: the mossy stones and well-kept gardens would make for great photos. But our vicar – so ancient he might as well be moss-covered too – once caught me in my first 'over-the-shirt fumble' moment in the bushes by the pond, so I'm not sure I could look him in the eye and promise to honour anything with my body, to be honest.

It's a great village. It has pretty much everything you need, if your needs aren't too extravagant. No holding your breath for a sushi bar, OK? It's always given me the things I need anyway. And I wouldn't change it for the world.

Except to make one addition, maybe. One not so small, glorious, unmissable addition. The one that makes me take that big gulp of air because looking down at our high street, I can see Flip has got a head start on me.

I've gone through the cupboard, into Narnia. Bunting Narnia. From the top of the hill, all I can see is bunting. Black and white bunting from lamppost to lamppost. Round litter bins and post boxes and traffic cones. Wrapped around and around and around again the oak trees by the pub. Wound through the railings by the pedestrian crossing. Across the Budgens awning. I can see Doreen trying to bring the shutter up but it's jammed. With bunting. It's like the bunting version of ivy, and someone's used an awful lot of fertiliser. Now this is a water cooler moment!

I stride to the first length of it, around the railings by the dog groomer's, Pet Power, and reach out my hand. It's a new form of bunting for us, not exactly durable but quick and cheap – both high priorities in our situation. Paper. So it hasn't been sewn, but stapled. And the paper it's been cut from says *SAVE BLUEBELL HALL!* over and over in big bold type, its message clear and unapologetic. Flip and I had thrashed the idea out over email when I'd shared that I wanted to take over the village with bunting in the way a flash mob takes over a train station. She instantly sent me a million images of yarn bombs and from there our bonkers but unmissable takeover began.

Flip said she'd produce all the bunting with her kids. A perfect rainy day project, plus teaching them all about the importance and power of community activism. I was imagining crayon-coloured triangles, roughly cut from newspaper and cereal boxes, but this is actually a beautiful art installation.

I leg it down to the library, where we had planned to meet. Flip is sitting on top of a litter bin, swinging her legs. The picture of innocence, bar the stapler and Sellotape in her hands. 'Don't be cross,' she grins sheepishly, 'but I just couldn't sleep, so I dragged Him Indoors out of bed at four a.m, left a note for the teen that she was in charge when they woke up, and we got a head start.'

I squeeze her in a death-grip hug. 'You are a Wonder Woman! Anything left to do, at all?!'

She surveys the street. 'Um, not really. Hubby's gone to get coffee from the garage, if you want one?'

I shake my head. 'This is… This is SO amazing. Better than I could have ever imagined. You're a legend!'

'You lay it out for me to play it out, boss lady.' She shrugs her shoulders happily. 'We PRs can spread the message, all right, but we don't make it. This was your baby. I just delivered it!' She instantly shivers. 'Urgh, I regret that metaphor.'

'Me too. But anyway, let's start spreading this particular message, shall we? I know a few peeps who will go especially bananas.'

I dig my phone out of my back pocket and send a message to the WhatsApp group: *If you go down to the shops today, you're sure of a big surprise…*

What?! Luce pings back.

I passed it on my way to work! Thumbs up, replies Dom.

> Flip has Bunting Bombed the village!
> Come see! Xxx

'I want you to mention in the interview that they should trademark that phrase to me, by the way,' Flip says, after reading over my shoulder.

I frown. 'Interview?'

'I just sent a picture over to the local press. They'll be here at eight a.m.!'

'Oh my god, really?! You beauty!' Our joint squeals must have woken up half of Hazlehurst. A thought makes me pull back.

'Christ, better wash my hair and put some non-smelly clothes on.'

Flip pinches her nose. 'Um, yes please. This is our media moment, dahling. You want to look whole-some, gorgeous, small-town but not uncivilised. That kind of a look.'

Flip obviously thinks way too much of my wardrobe. I will probably settle for my best cashmere jumper, the one without the moth hole. 'Right. See you later then, hun? And in case I didn't make it clear, you are THE best!'

As I race back home for a wash up and a rehearsal of some good sound bites, I pass – of all people – arsing Alex Granger, out for a run in his tech stretchy gear. Annoyingly, he doesn't look a complete berk in it like most of the male joggers around here – it's showing off his toned legs and his muscly arms. But even The Suit can't kill my buzz.

His eyes flick down to my t-shirt as he jogs past and his pace slows, but he's not having a minute of this day.

'Do head down to the village,' I say airily, 'for some real community spirit.'

Flip's right. This is our moment. And it feels great.

Chapter 10

There's nothing so humbling as squeezing your adult-sized, biscuit-padded bum onto a child's chair, no matter if days before you were part of a local media coup. I'm smooshing my way along the row, my hand-coloured programme clutched in front of me, to the seat Luce has saved.

'Just in time!' she whispers. 'Steve would never have forgiven you if you'd missed his revolving carrot crops. They're old loo roll tubes that we spent a night paper-maché-ing.'

'Remind me again why it's so bad to be single? I just watch box sets and drink wine for kicks, poor old single me.'

'Ha ha. But you're not sorry we spent one of our lust-filled nights of frenzy making this lot?' She points at the red and brown bunting tacked up along the front of the school hall stage. I know just how it's been created, as Steve talked me through it at great length, with a weird amount of pride. He had pinched some felt from his school stores, a glue gun and garden twine, so that made the ballast of his bunting. Then tails of fake fur were glue-gunned onto the point of each triangle. It was really effective, if a bit cheaty. When I teased him for skipping out on any sewing he merely stated: those who can, do. Those who can't, glue gun. Fair enough. It looks brilliant and fits right in with the rest of the *Fantastic Mr Fox* decor around the hall. Masks and signs and sketches, all made by the class.

The audience of parents and children do a collective sssshhhh and shuffle in their seats, as Steve appears from between the thick stage curtains.

I bite my lip, as hard as I can bear, to stop myself from laughing. This is the guy I once memorised 'Slam Dunk Da Funk' with, pausing and rewinding a VHSed episode of *Top of the Pops* until we had the lyrics and dance moves sadly perfect. And now he's an educator. It's all a bit ridiculous.

But Luce's eyes are shining with pride as Steve addresses the tightly packed space and so I do my best to find some awe.

'Ladies and gentlemen and pupils!' He claps his hands and then rubs them together, in the way all male teachers mysteriously do. 'Welcome to Year Five's production of *Fantastic Mr Fox*. I hope none of you have food in your pockets because our foxes have incredible noses for sniffing things out.'

And all of a sudden a handful of small children in brown leotards and painted fox masks come slinking down the aisle, sniffing at people's jackets and eliciting tiny, happy shrieks from little pupils on the way.

'Before we start the show, I hope you've been admiring my lovely fox bunting here.' He takes a step back. 'It was made by the Bluebell Bunting Society, who no doubt you've all been reading about in the paper today.' There was a ripple of murmurs around me and a tingle of excitement shot up my spine. 'If you want to find out more about them, and the great Sunday Fundays at the Hall, where you can do lots of crafty projects like this bunting, come and see me afterwards for a flier.'

Another hand rub, and Steve winked in our direction. 'Lights please!'

The one spotlight dimmed and a lot of badly concealed whispering could be heard behind the wings. 'Clara. Clara! First line! Where's your blummin' tail?'

–

'It's at times like these that I remember I should never complain about my job.' Lucy pulls her loose cardi tightly around her middle, as we huddle by the school's gates and wait for Steve to come out. If I hadn't just seen him chase a maverick, bum-wiggling farmer across the stage for ten minutes, I could fool myself that we were fifteen and about to go and hang at the park. But we're twenty-nine and we're going for a Harvester. Which my fifteen-year-old self would have been super impressed with and thought pretty posh. Who am I kidding, the current me is salivating at the thought of a mountain of ribs.

It wasn't a bad show, per se. You're never going to get a West End chorus at these things, but I think Steve may have been optimistic about the running time. The kids, the audience and the sets were starting to droop at thirty minutes in and at forty-seven minutes all hell broke loose when Kevin Veevers decided to make his own fun and yell, somewhat existentially I thought, 'It's not real, you know. It's just a boring play! I haven't even had my tea yet!'

Steve eventually jogs towards us, letting out a lungful of air in a long, exasperated sigh. 'The usual complaints about not enough solo time for Timothy, but then a lot of questions about the Hall. All good stuff – you might have a packed Sunday Funday this weekend.'

'I really hope so. I'm kind of counting on it. And hopefully people still read the *Shires Bugle*, and that might send hundreds of visitors our way. We've only got twelve days to go. Now the appeal has been shot down by The Suit, I've got to hit that visitor number. Pronto.'

Lucy leans into Steve as he wraps his arm around her middle. It's a movement so fluid and familiar, I don't think either of them are aware they're doing it. 'I haven't seen the paper. Was it good coverage?'

'Well, it just so happens...' I dig the three pristine, ironed copies of the *Bugle* out of my hold-all. Mum made me promise to get one copy for her, one copy for me, and one for best. I think she wants to frame it. This hasn't happened since I won the school prize for Geography in year eight.

Lucy flips it open and takes in the huge photo on the front page. It dominates almost the whole thing: bunting fluttering in the breeze on the high street in the foreground, more bunting and a few bemused faces in the background. 'Wow. Great headline too, Con!'

Bunting Bomb Hits Hazlehurst! It's a bit of old school clickbait, but I love it. And Flip is over the moon that her new phrase is taking off. The subheading reads: *Local community take over village in protest over Bluebell Hall closure.* Why yes, we are taking over. Thank you. We're kicking butt.

Lucy's eyes scan further down into the article and she suddenly sucks in her breath and says 'Ouch!'

'What?'

'You named The Suit in your interview? Um, OK. That's pretty bold.'

I shrug with more confidence than I feel. I had a been a bit hyped up when chatting to the journalist, overcome with the sight of our bunting filling the street and pumped with adrenalin from rushing home and back. She'd asked me what locals could do to get behind us and after I'd said we wanted to see them all at the Hall for one of our excellent events, I felt a nasty twinge of revenge. Like a little red devil on my shoulder, telling me: might as well stick it to the mansplainer, while we have the chance! So I added, 'And if you feel strongly, as I do, that losing our local heritage for business profits is a crying shame, please do get in contact with Alex Granger at the Hibbert Estate to voice your concerns.'

Steve pumps his fist in the air. 'Power to the people. Down with the man!'

'Exactly! I didn't say he smells or anything. I just pointed out what his role in this is and how people could talk to him.'

'OK?' Luce doesn't look at all convinced. 'I suppose he is the bad guy. Even if he is just doing his job.'

I shove my hands in my back pockets. 'And I'm just doing mine.'

'And I'm done with mine for another ten hours so let's eat ribs while the sun shines. I need a post-show cider, where none of the parents can see me and find me and ask me about doing Bugsy Sodding Malone again.' Steve throws his arm along my shoulders and steers us both towards the car.

–

There's an extra boost of energy to the Bunting Society when we next meet, for the first time after the newspaper went out. Not just that we took over the town for the day and made the papers, but that the Village Committee have officially pledged their support for our cause and want us to play a big part in the May Day fete. We're going to supply the bunting, of course, but also have a tent of our very own, to showcase the wonderful history of the Hall as part of the village and let everyone know what they can come and do there. We're going to go nuts with the tent's decoration, naturally, and deck it out with the weirdest and wildest bunting we can think of to really catch the eye. And it couldn't come at a better time – the May Day fete is just a handful of days away from the deadline and I'm hoping it will give us a boost of attendance to take us over our target. My fingers are so tightly crossed I'm worried they'll never untangle.

At the start of tonight's meeting, I declared it a free-for-all and put out my stack of pencils and pads for sketching and brainstorming for the fete display. As everyone gets down to scribbling and drawing, in between sips of tea, Flip is moving around the room, pointing her iPhone at anything and everything she can.

'How's it going with the social media domination?'

Flip pauses to fiddle with the silk scarf tied around her lush red hair. 'Not too shabby, not at all. Content coming along nicely. Helps that we have such gorgeous stitchers!' She pauses to wink at Susannah who laughs and bats her away. 'I'm just glad you sweet-talked our student girls into running the Twitter and Facebook accounts. I mean, I thought I had a handle on this stuff but…'

'Hey,' I give her a little squeeze on the arm, 'they were literally born with cries that took up no more than 140 characters – we might as well harness their crazy youth. I'm a Facebook girl, but old school. I mostly lurk these days. But I do know that done right, it can be brilliant for bringing groups together and sharing inspirational stories. So I wanted some experts. It just so happens they're seventeen. So we'll get the great content, they do the good sharing.'

Flip looks uncharacteristically deflated for a brief moment. 'But even a year ago, in London, I was totally hot on my social media. It just moves so fast. Anyway, I've got all these from installing the Bunting Bomb.' She swipes back and shows me her husband up a ladder against Budgens, looking half asleep as he ties bunting around a hanging basket holder in the dawn light. 'And then these from when we took it down and recycled it properly.' With a few more swipes, we're looking at her man again, but this time gleefully shoving handfuls of bunting into a giant paper recycling bin. 'With some action shots of bunting business tonight, that gives us a bold start. Oh, I love a good opportunistic campaign!' She's recovered her bounce and her grin is so wide it almost smudges her lipstick.

'I don't know what I'd do without you, Flip. You are a star. You've made this whole thing happen.'

She gives a quick curtesy. 'A total pleasure, Connie. Total. But I'm just the noisemaker: you made the message for me to spread, remember.'

Being British, I never quite know how to take a compliment so I mutter something about restocking the bobbins and wander off.

Everyone has their heads down over a sketchbook or rummaging in one of our big IKEA bags of fabric offcuts, so with no one to help, I think I might do a quick totalising of our log book. Sunday Funday this weekend should really make the difference, now we've had a mention at the school and through the paper.

As I fetch the book from the hallway, I spot that Dom has moved off, to sit alone in a quiet corner. Tonight's rugby shirt is baggy through being worn almost to death, and his skin is tinged with grey.

'Hello stranger! No Polly tonight?'

He grunts. 'No. With 'friends' is all I'm told. And the curfew gets ignored too. So I've decided not just to sit in and wait like a mug. I've come out, take my mind off things. Enjoy myself.' But the mobile on his lap, which his eyes dart back to every twenty seconds, says otherwise.

A disappearing teen doesn't sound good, but it's way beyond my level of experience. 'Oh. Right. I'm sure she'll be home bang on time tonight.'

Another grunt.

'Had any good ideas?'

He turns his empty paper to face me. 'I'm not a fabrics kind of man, if I'm honest. Precise cutting up, measuring, yes. But creative flair, not on your nelly. Flip's paper bunting, that's more my bag. Quick and efficient. I might make some for the restaurant. But I'm not your arty sort. Polly got that from her mother.' He picks up his phone and presses the button to wake it up. No messages.

I'm suddenly feeling very tongue-tied. How do you jolly someone who's lost their life partner, the mother of their child? I can do scraped knees and sweeping up biscuit crumbs. But this kind of fix feels so far beyond me I can't even imagine what it looks like.

'Polly's project – how did that go down with Miss Ingram?'

He closely inspects the ceiling. 'Good, good. Turns out the teacher hadn't been briefed on Polly's... background. So she didn't know when she set the family tree theme just how hard that was for Pol.'

'And for you.'

'Well, yes. There's that.' He shifts on the hard plastic seat. 'I didn't know what to say when she brought it out, the cut up bits of her mum's stuff. I... it caught me off guard. Don't get me wrong, it's beautiful. And Sue would have loved it. Sue. That was my wife's name.'

I nod. Hoping he'll go on.

'I just... I thought I should maybe save all her things, the way they were. For Polly, when she was older. She might want them. And I didn't want the house to change, not straight away. I wanted Polly to still recognise it as her home.'

I crouch down and sit against the wall by Dom's chair. 'It'll always be her home, because you're there. It was just me and Mum growing up, and I never felt anything but at home with her. And it wasn't all tea and crumpets. There were times that were hard and we fell out. But we always came back together.'

'Really?' Dom's face is suddenly lit up with so much hope, it's like I've just shown him the last life jacket on the Titanic. 'She sometimes goes off all day on a weekend, sometimes she doesn't get back till late after school. It's hard when you're trying to figure out the best way forward on your own.'

I nod.

'You know that dream where it's ten minutes before a Physics exam and you haven't got a pen and all you can remember is two French verbs? Parenting is like that. All the time.' He gives a half-hearted smile.

I stand up and brush off my jeans. 'Well, you're clearly doing a great job. Because that girl is wonderful. That idea she had about the art therapy class? That's was so selfless and kind and mature. I was blown away. She's a credit to you. And I personally love a bit of feistiness in a teenage girl. Shows they'll be able to fend for themselves in life.'

Dom fiddles with his phone again. 'Hmm.' I think he is also very British about accepting compliments.

'I'm going to get you a tea and we're going to put your talents to better use. We'll need some signage printed for the tent. Do you know anyone who could do that on the cheap?

'Actually, yes. I do know a bloke. I'll give him a ring.'

'Brilli—'

I'm cut off by a shrill scream. Oh god. Someone's caught a major artery with the pinking shears.

'Conniiiiiiiiiie!' Flip yells, and rushes over, Susannah hot on her heels with a shocked look. 'It's big… It's… Oh my god!'

I grab her by the forearms. 'Is anyone bleeding out?!'

'No, no, but we are on fire!'

'Who! Who's on fire?!'

'The campaign. I've just had an email from the *Mirror*. They want to pick up the regional story, with more colour. Everyone needs good news stories right now. I've told them to come to the May Day fete. Eeeeep!' She bounces on the spot, round and round in circles.

Susannah claps behind her. 'It's so wonderful! A national newspaper, no less! I'm going to call your mum.' Flip and I dance about together before spreading the news to the rest of the society.

'This is it, people!' I shout happily. 'Bluebell Hall is on the up! We need bunting like there's no tomorrow!'

Chapter 11

The Bluebells all ooohed and aaaahed at my paint job in the hall at the last meeting but tonight we're moving outside, onto the scrubby patch of ground behind the building. With everything that's been going on, I perhaps haven't been the most attentive Bloom Mistress. One of our meetings recently was themed 'modern journalism' and I got them comparing a copy of *Heat* to the home page of *BuzzFeed*. For ninety minutes, with some squash for kicks.

But now we seem to be on a high with our campaign and everything is about nailing the perfect May Day fete, just nine days away, so I really do need to catch up with my girls and their part of the day – maypole dancing. Yup, skipping round a log with some gaudy ribbons. It's still happening in this day and age. And I'm perpetrating it.

I always felt like a prat doing maypole dances when I was a Bluebell but Gran wouldn't hear of us moving on to something different. Even the mention of Scottish Country dancing instead had her tsking and rolling her eyes. To be fair, she used to play the accordion for us herself and the memory of her elbows and shoulders swinging back and forth, a massive grin plastered on her wrinkly face, is still one of my most vivid childhood memories. So I'm sticking firmly in the past with Gran on this one.

We don't get the actual pole out to practise with (I'm not the Incredible Caretaker. I can barely lift the old cassette player out of its box, let alone a trussed up caber) but we have the crown of ribbons from the top, and that sits on a traffic cone while I hit play on my crunchy-sounding tape of accordion music. Some of the girls here have a few May Day fetes behind them and know the drill of keeping up with the pace of the song but not overtaking anyone in a flush of excitement and bodging up the pattern. Veronica is my maypole Jedi Knight. If I ever pause while yelling out instructions, she calmly takes up where I left off. 'Pass on your left, skip back twice, and around.' And all the Bluebells fall into a perfectly synchronised jig. Sometimes I think I should just abdicate and make her Bloom Mistress right now, before she cuts me in half with a lightsaber.

Gurpreet is struggling a bit with left and right today, something I'm familiar with, so we tuck a pencil between the laces of her right trainer. 'You write with a pencil. So you write on your right,' I say for the tenth time. She gives me a sunny thumbs up and clutches her green ribbon like a tug of war is about to break out.

'Nice and gentle, now off we go!' The music crackles into life. It's the song that goes, 'I want to be near you, you're the one the one the one. I want to be near you, you're the one for me.'

My heart suddenly feels a bit full and bursting with thoughts of Gran. She would have loved this. I mean, not Gurpreet going the wrong way, but the music and the girls and general life at the Hall. It's going to be all right, Gran, I think. I'm fixing it for you. For everyone. Just wait and see.

After five more minutes we're in a right tangle, so I call a break and send the girls to stretch. Because this is a serious sporting pursuit and I won't have anyone say it's not.

Without being asked, Veronica picks up a few ribbon ends and joins me in unweaving the big lumpy mess they've become. 'Miss, can I ask you a few things about the Scouts?'

'Um, sure.' Maybe Veronica has her first crush?

'Are they really as awful as they seem?'

I wince. 'How awful do they seem to you, currently?'

'Pretty awful. It's just, if we are going to share their hut, I think I'd better prepare myself for that now. Let it sink in.' A tiny shudder makes her shoulders wobble.

I unstick a red from a green and put a purple back where it came from. 'Why on earth would you share their hut?'

She waves a casual hand at the Hall. 'When this place is torn down.'

'Veronica!'

She colours a little as she realises this is perhaps a sensitive issue for someone employed by this Hall and very much counting on it not being torn down.

In a small voice she explains, 'Gemma's brother is a Scout. He said over tea that the Scout Master had asked them all to be extra welcoming to us Bluebells as we were shortly about to lose our premises, to make way for a new building. We'd have to share with them. I thought you knew. I assumed you must have known.'

My nails are suddenly making deep crescent shapes in the wide nylon ribbons. 'That's not happening, Veronica. That's just a pile of… silly rumours.'

'But Gemma said her brother said the Scout Master said he works for the people that own the Hall so—'

'So he can kiss my arse,' I breathe.

Veronica's eyebrows huddle above her nose. 'Sorry, Miss?'

'Why don't we get off this damp grass?' I singsong brightly, pushing my rage down, right down, to the bottom of my trainers.

The anger at what arrogant BS Alex has been drilling into his mini-me army has me so furiously bristling that I'm verging on a full beard of rage.

The suit-wearing rat.

Anger keeps me fuelled through the week, as I listen to The OAP Three sing completely different songs with big grins on their faces. I nod along, feeling too sorry for them, their deaf ears and their holey memories to correct them and too busy picturing how I might run Alex through with a tent pole to find the polite words, anyway. My ancient little pop group are going to sing songs from back in the day at our Bluebell Hall memories tent – the less creepy Victorian children's songs and cheery WW2 numbers. 'Pack Up Your Troubles'? Alex can pack his bags and catch the next loser bus out of Hazlehurst, thanks very much.

Flip has been giving me 'media training' ahead of meeting the *Mirror* at the fete next weekend. She bumped into me when picking Gurpreet up again after the Bluebell tangle-athlon and I was still so white-hot with rage that you could have cooked a potato waffle on my forehead. I think she's a bit worried that the 'human interest' piece might go a bit 'human remains found at fete' if I see Alex there, so we're meeting at the Handsome Hog for a G&T and some more polishing of my sound bite. It took me a while to shake off my embarrassment at drinking at the Handsome Hog when I came back from Manchester, at first. You never think the pub you try (and fail) to sneak into when you're fifteen will be the one you legitimately frequent when it's… God, fifteen years later! That was half my lifetime ago.

As I sip my drink and kill time waiting for Flip, I snap a quick picture for Stevie. The caption underneath says:

They ran out of snakebite apparently. Shame.

He replies:

> Still can't believe you tried to convince the barman that you were your own older cousin from High Wycombe. You delivered his papers to him every Sunday, you div!!! And stop sending me pics of sexy looking G&Ts when I'm in bed with numeracy marking and an Ovaltine.

> You were more fun when you were underage.

> That is the kind of text that makes a teacher sweat. Night, Connie.

Flip's red barnet hops into sight around one of the pub's etched glass partitions. It's the kind of pub where they weren't fancy enough to rip all this original stuff out in the eighties and through sheer dumb luck it's now trendy again. Last week as I ate a cheeky pub burger for my lunch, I overheard some guys with topknots saying in awe, 'totally legit place, shame there's no craft beers.' So, some more ex-Londoners for our population, then. Bless them and their disposable cash.

'Hey chuck!' She shuffles along next to me on the padded bench. 'Sorry I'm late. My big girl had a toxic friend situation. Blerg.' She mimes two fingers going down her throat.

'Oh no. Is she OK?'

Flip shrugs. 'Nothing a good cry, some mango sorbet and a read of Caitlyn Moran can't cure.'

Not for the first time I'm glad I haven't had to go through puberty in this tech age. All we had as a fall back in my day was the Spice Girls and a

Wagon Wheel. If you were lucky. If I'd been shamed or trolled or whatever as a teen, I think I would have slung my phone in the pond and gone to live a hermit's life in the woods. I might not have smelled pretty, but at least the mean girls wouldn't have been able to find me. No 4G in those woods.

Flip claps her hands together. 'But onwards and upwards. Let's get you ready for the camera!' She catches my flinch. 'You've nothing to be scared of, Cons. You're smart and motivated, and pretty easy on the eye. Newspaper eds' jackpot, I'd say. I can't convince you to come in a bikini?'

I choke on my ice cube just as she belts out her throaty laugh. 'Kidding!'

When I clear my airwaves, I croak, 'So shall we rehearse what I'm going to say?'

'Oh no. You don't want it to sound all formal and stuffy. It has to be from the heart, off the cuff. But we can have a bit of role play, so you roughly get the gist of what you might say. I'll be the journo, you be you.'

'Right. Well, at least I can do that.'

Flip coughs a little and positions her hands like she has a little tape recorder under my chin. 'Miss Duncan, tell us about the plight of Bluebell Hall. What does it mean to the community here?'

'Um, well, um. Yes. It's a really vital part of Hazle-hurst life. The local girls' group, the Bluebells, meet there, which gives vital confidence and social skills to girls from all walks of life. Yup.'

With a roll of her hands, Flip encourages me to keep talking. 'And we have some local OAPs who see us weekly. They don't otherwise get out or have any contact apart from Meals on Wheels, so it's a lifeline to them. Also, local families' use the drop-in sessions on Sunday Fundays as a free bit of activity and engagement for their children. All free services, of course. And you don't get much free these days, with this government.'

Flip chops at her neck. 'Too heavy! No politics,' she mouths. I wonder if she knows her Dictaphone is imaginary?

'Ahhh, um. We do all sorts – arts, crafts, singing, dancing. And of course, we make bunting!' I do an air-hostess-like point around me. Christ, now I'm fully down this role play rabbit hole. Can't wait to read this edition of the '*Daydream Mirror*' when it comes out.

'The bunting is great.' Flip winks, so I must have done something right. 'It's certainly caught everyone's attention.'

'It shows what you can achieve when you get together with your neighbours. Not the sort of thing you'll see if we're torn down for a megabucks coffee house, or something. That's the rumour.'

'And you have a credible source for that?'

'I should say so. From the guy representing the Hibbert estate himself. He told me. If we don't get enough locals to use the Hall they're going to sell it off and destroy it. All that history, all those families losing out.' Suddenly I can feel a heavy lump behind my ribs but Flip gives me a thumbs up.

'And when is your deadline? When will you know the fate of Bluebell Hall?'

'The Monday following this fete, in fact. We're hoping everyone will see our tent, or read about it somewhere, and come along on Bank Holiday Monday for a special Monday Funday. If nobody uses the Hall, we'll lose it. That's why we want all your readers to come along. That should give us the numbers we need to satisfy the fat cats.' I spit the last bit out, imagining a boardroom full of cats dressed in fancy suits and goring cute little mice.

With an imaginary flick to her non-existent recorder, Flip sits back and beams. 'Really good! Giving them that sense of urgency will hopefully mean we make it into the Sunday edition. Ooh, forgot they'll want background colour on you.' She leans forward again, lowering her brows. 'Tell us a bit about yourself, Connie.'

'Um, I work at the Hall. I'm the caretaker.'

'And?' Wobbling her head, Flip somehow communicates she's losing interest.

'And, I'll, er, be thirty next month. I've lived here all my life, apart from when I temped in Manchester, after uni.'

'Right, so what was your career plan, before the Hall came along?'

I shake my head, a flicker of memories of the *B-Side* office passing before my eyes and quickly vanishing again. 'Sorry?'

Flip leans forward and whispers, 'They'll want that little intro line of you. You know 'Flip Gooderson, forty-three, mother of three, a former PR from London, now a WI member and sewing enthusiast in the Shires'. So you'd be 'Connie Duncan, a...'

I chew on my bottom lip. 'I suppose, twenty-nine, a Philosophy graduate. Single. Who lives with her mum?'

She winces like she's just seen the barman spit in a pint. 'You couldn't add 'aspiring...?'

'Aspiring to keep the community hall open. There.'

'There's nothing else you want to do?'

'No. Why? This is where I live, this is my big passion. You know that, Flip.'

She fiddles with a strand of hair that's come loose from her up-do. 'Well, yes. But... it's not what you dream of at eighteen, is it? No offence. But once we've saved the Hall, once this media campaign is everywhere, just think what an amazing jumping-off point that could be for you! You could get into PR yourself, or event management, move back to a big city, stop hanging out with boring old married ladies like me...' She rolls her eyes and smiles. But suddenly I'm not feeling very jolly.

I feel shaky, like I'm at a job interview I didn't even apply for. The pressure starts to make my head ache. 'Not everyone wants what you've had, Flip. Hazlehurst isn't a second choice, OK? It's where my home is, where everyone I love is. And I'm not sure how this has anything to do with saving the Hall, actually. So... Yeah, thanks for the help. I need an early night.'

I grab my denim jacket and leave the bar doors flapping behind me, Flip's white face just visible in small bursts as they open and close.

She couldn't know that she'd hit on the exact same argument I'd been having with myself for weeks now.

Chapter 12

With everything going on, this art therapy class is just what I need. Not only because it's bringing a gaggle of new visitors to the Hall, not only because it's Polly's idea and she's shown real passion and flair in getting it off the ground, but because I think I could do with a little emotional release of my own. Our campaign is charging ahead, and I'm charging along with it, but every now and then when I pause for breath and to hoover up five bits of buttery toast, I can feel the weight of the Hall on me. I can feel the Bunting Society looking to me for the next idea, I can feel the total number of visitors so far hanging over me at every turn. The closer we get to our target, weirdly, the more stressed I become from all the expectation. Sometimes I even feel like Gran is just over my shoulder, crossing her fingers that I won't let her or Hibbert down.

So a little sewing, a little cutting and sticking, a little light conversation over tea and Jammie Dodgers is just what the doctor ordered.

Polly is twirling a length of pea-green ribbon round and round her hands in the kitchen when I seek her out.

'Hey teach!' I put my hand up for a high five but Polly just looks at it, numb with panic. 'You OK?'

'Um, yeah. I suppose. No. No, not really.'

I fiddle about with teacups and beakers. 'This is going to be great, I just know it. How could it not be?'

She shoves her hands into the back pockets of her cobalt-blue jeans. 'Easy for you to say. You're awesome at this stuff. You can talk to people, new people, weird people. I just… I don't know what to say. I got all excited about doing this textiles things, to get visitors here to the Hall. And I didn't actually realise that I'd have to talk to them, you know?'

The memory of my first ever session as Mistress Bloom comes flooding back. The stammering. The sweat patches. The seven cups of chamomile it took to finally calm down afterwards. 'Yup, I do know. But I also know you have it in you. Because there is really only one trick to talking to new people.'

Polly's hands wave in front of her grimacing mug. 'Eww, not the imagining them in underwear thing, please. Please! There are old people waiting out there!'

'Nope. Talking to people is like a treasure hunt. Everyone has at least one super interesting story to them – you just have to keep digging until you find it. Some people will have little nuggets of gold to them, others will have big shiny diamonds as big as your head. Just keep going till you strike it rich.' I nudge her in the ribs. 'Besides, once we start crafting, people tend to lose themselves in satin stitch quite happily.'

She takes a big gulp of squash from a scratched beaker. 'OK. OK.'

'And,' I lower my voice as the A-levellers from the Bunting Society approach the kitchen. I know with a few years on Polly and three sets of piercings apiece, they are uber-cool in her eyes and she wouldn't want them to know just how nervous she's feeling. 'If it all goes tits up, give me a wink and I'll flash my boobs. Never fails to change the subject.'

Her eyes go wide and she bites back a giggle. 'Here's hoping I don't just get something in my eye, then. Hey Clara, hey Bernie.'

Polly is smashing her first go at public speaking.

'So really, it doesn't matter what kind of sewing experience you have. Here at Sew Chill the idea isn't to make something perfect. It's to make something that reflects you. Who you are, where you came from. Where you want to go. We're going to start with a community quilt. Everyone here can make a square about happiness – more than one, if you like – then us lot will join them up,' she says, pointing her thumb in the direction of the A-level girls who nod encouragingly, 'and… and I thought we could then auction it off for,' her voice wobbles a little, 'cancer research.'

Spontaneous applause breaks out around the tables.

Polly recovers with a quick cough. 'It's totally fine just to work on ideas this week, you don't have to rush into anything. But if you do want to have a go at something, we have fabrics, needles, thread. Books on craft. All the stuff you need. You could hand-sew, use a machine, layer materials, go as nuts as you like. Or you can bring in materials from home next week, things that means something special. I made this,' her cheeks flush as she holds up her family tree bunting, 'from clothes and bits that had been my mum's. Um, yeah, so just to say again: I'm Polly. Please shout if you need help. And, um…'

Bernie rescues her by chipping in, 'Have fun guys! Welcome to Sew Chill!'

'Hasn't she done well? Sweet thing,' Mum murmurs as she starts pulling out a tangle of fabric offcuts. I'm so pleased she was up for coming tonight. The Hall is in our shared DNA, so it's great to have her part of its new lease of life. She belongs here.

But, more than that, I think the sewing will be great for her – relaxing, distracting and positive. I hadn't realised Polly had had the brainwave of us making a quilt for charity but it's so perfect. This club will help the people in it find a bit more balance and also do something for the greater good. Shame I didn't meet Polly when she was younger – she could have been a star Bluebell. I could have just put my feet up and let her think of all the community outreach projects for the Help a Neighbour badge.

Mum is comparing some yellow gingham to a scrap of orange velvet. 'I'm thinking a sun for happiness. Holidays. Do these go? I could do triangles all sewn together in a round to make a big sun face.'

'That sounds nice. How do you think I could patchwork a tube of Pringles and the Netflix logo?'

Mum mimes jabbing me with her needle. 'Shush. Don't you dare. I remember when you had that denim jacket and you embroidered lovely things on it. What were you, 11? Gran helped you with it and you got your handicrafts badge.'

I press my hand to my mouth. I hadn't thought of that jacket in a decade. But back then it was my pride and joy. A simple New Look number, I'd bought it with my pocket money then Gran had helped me out with haberdashery supplies: embroidery floss, a special transfer pen and a few sequinned patches. She helped me plan out the design, draw it onto baking parchment with the pen then give it a good iron so the drawing went onto the denim. Then it was up to me and three weeks of feverish sewing by my desk lamp to complete it. There were huge wonky sunflowers all over the back, a row of Take That symbols along the bottom hem and the sequinny butterflies floating up the right side of the jacket. God, it was a mess. But I loved it.

'I wonder if it's in the loft somewhere? Shame I stopped being a size eight a long time ago.'

Mum's eyes mist over and she smiles down into the triangle stencil she's cutting. 'Your Gran was so proud of how hard you worked on it. She told me we should send you to a fashion school.'

'Me?! Me, who once wore a lime green Lycra top with muddy brown cords to a school disco?'

Mum laughs, but not unkindly. 'She thought you could do anything. She said you had rightly inherited the female Duncan genes that made you an unstoppable one-man-band.' She nods decisively, as if these were actual genes recently mapped by scientists in white coats and goggles.

Not so much a one-man-band as a no man's land when it comes to my love life, Gran, I thought as Mum pushed the box of material my way. Something about the conversation I'd had with Flip at the pub (well, the heated bit of it, anyway) had stirred up a lot of memories of Dell. And when I pushed those aside, it left me with the realisation that he was probably the last guy I'd gone out with. And that was four years ago. Maybe once the Hall was safe and sound, I could get one of the A–Level girls to talk me through Tinder. Slowly. But that was definitely a topic for another time. Not one to be shared with my mum over pin cushions.

I found a chintzy print in a soft, powdery blue. 'Bluebells. Maybe I can copy a picture off my phone. Seeing as my awful mother didn't send me to fashion school so now I'm hopeless at drawing. Chuh.'

'Oh, it's always the mother's fault,' Mum says with mock weariness and catches Susannah's eye. They nod in unison, then Susannah goes back to stitching and nattering with two of the ladies from her retirement village. Their work looks enviably neat.

I decide on stitching the word Bluebells on the chintzy fabric as actually sketching the flower seems a bit beyond me and it could easily be confused for a bunch of grapes in my inexpert hands. Though I'm sure, to someone out there, grapes mean happiness. But I'd always rather have the Pringles.

The next thing I know, I'm chaining stitching round the second 'b' without even realising a minute has gone by, let alone twenty. For the first time in weeks, my brain hasn't been buzzing and twitching with new worries or ideas, nothing about the past or the future is troubling me, it has just happily sat here as I threaded my needle, softly pushing the point in and out, in and out, following the lines of my task. This stuff works!

As I surface slowly from my sewing meditation and look around me, I can see the huddle of faces, bent over notebooks or sewing hoops. Each face wears a matching look of inner calm and utter tranquility. And with my brain now operating at a healthy speed, I can take stock of what's really going on here. Yes, new visitors have been clocked up tonight and that makes me happy. But more than that, much more, is that we are using this Hall for exactly the purpose it was built for: the village is coming together, sharing skills, sharing problems. Right here, surrounded by stray buttons and tangles of ribbon, we've made a little Hazlehurst Eden and it's for anyone who wants to join in. No money needed, no status, no qualifications. This is why Hibbs built up this Hall and this is why I'm going to fight for it.

Chapter 13

'Mmm, I love the smell of poster paint in the morning!' Steve stands with his hands on his hips, a smudge of blue on the seat of his sandy-coloured cords. Seeing as he's at the fete today in a school capacity, he's in full-on respectable teacher uniform.

There is so much to get done before the fete kicks off at ten, I'd persuaded Steve and Luce (and Abel) to make a sort of picnic breakfast out of it as we got our bits and pieces together in the park. I guess I might have painted a rosy Famous Five type picture, when in fact I've brought Sainsbury's croissants and a flask of tea that's getting that weird metallic taste. And I forgot the blanket, so our legs are a bit wet.

Steve and his family troupe are painting big signs for the Hall's tent: *Make Your Own Bunting Here! Read About Local History! Join The Bluebells!* And then what I think is a yellow dinosaur dancing with a pig. That's from Abel. We're just letting him go free range for a bit.

I'm getting to grips with the gazebo. Susannah managed to borrow it from her retirement home but neglected to mention it had about 700 pole pieces and no instructions, just random red triangles and blue squares on the end of things. What makes trying to stupidly shove one pole into the end of another pole when it clearly doesn't feel like it even worse, is that all around me other tents and awnings are popping up in mere seconds, marking the perimeter of the fete.

I huffily kick at the peg bag and then try not to squeal as my toes take the impact. Stupid stupid stupid.

'It's fine to ask for help,' Steve says in a calm voice, splodging a smiley face on some white card. 'I'm sure one of those other tent guys could give it a go with you.'

I bat the idea away with my free hand, the one not clutching four different metal poles. 'I'm fine. I can do it.'

'Getting help is not the same as not being able to do it. It's just sensible. Because according to your schedule, you wanted this thing up by now and half the bunting in place. But it's your call.' He rubs at his chin. I'm not going to tell him he's just smooshed bright red paint into his stubble. He can find out when his pupils arrive.

'Morning!' Brian, the Village Committee chairman, bounds over, his bum bag slapping against his waterproof trousers. 'Does anyone need a hand?'

Without catching Steve's eye, because I know it will be smug, I let the poles clatter to my feet. 'Me please.'

It's one of those confusing bright but cloudy days, where you want to squint because of the sharp light but to put your sunglasses on would look a bit daft, there not being any visible sun or anything. But I think that's just about perfect for a fete – not too hot, not too cold, perfect mooching weather to take in a dog show, waste a fiver on the tombola to win some Radox, and even absorb some local history with a social crusade on the side.

The Bunting Society has outdone itself: the inside of our gazebo is not so much Middle England dream as Middle Eastern harem – the bunting is swagged along the walls, back and forth along the ceiling, tucked in around the poles. There are bright colours, bold patterns, clashes of beautiful things, artfully done. We've got pennants made of felt with fuzzy felt decorations, we've got knitted and crocheted pennants, and we've even got a string of the paper bunting left over from our takeover of the village. The Sew Chill group have their finished charity quilt pinned up – it really is an object of happiness; amazing that it came together in a week – and are doing a roaring trade with the raffle tickets to win it. It's like being in a lush greenhouse where all the vines and creepers and flowers are actually made out of fabric and bias binding and string. I love it. I'm buzzing with pride.

My buzz helps me sidestep any weirdness with Flip when she arrives. I never pegged her as a 'Settle down, young lady' type but her questioning the other night really rankled me. OK, I might not have a grand life plan. But who said I have to? And anyway, today is not about that: today is about selling the back legs off the Hall to anyone who'll listen. Including the press. So I'm putting any awkwardness from that drink to the back of our mind as we tackle the matter at hand.

'Ready?' She asks gingerly, putting down a wicker basket behind our table.

I give a double thumbs up – the international hand gesture for ultimate confidence. 'What's in the basket?'

'Flapjacks. Oat and raisin cookies. Diet Coke. Fuel to keep us going all day long!' She rocks back and forth on her emerald green ballet shoes. 'What time do the Bluebells go on? Gurpreet told me, but then she went into the plot of *Frozen* in a lot of detail and I got sidetracked.'

My eyes wander to the performance area smack bang in the middle of the park. 'Noon. The big show.' I grimace.

'They'll be fine!'

'Probably. I'm actually more nervous about the maypole than the Hall, to be honest. I know people won't be able to help but love what we've got going on here. But whether we'll keep the locals entertained with fifteen minutes of knotted up ribbons is another matter. Next year, I'm going to blow the budget and get a live accordion player. Actually, I'm going to start rounding them up. That could take a good hour, especially if the doughnut stall has opened. Are you OK here? Give me a bell if the journalist turns up.'

'Will do. Have fun!'

-

Luce has been politely swallowing her hysteria as I take the Bluebells through an improvised warm-up. It's based on what I can remember from a *Geordie Shore* exercise DVD Steve gave me as a gag gift and a Pilates class that Mum and I went to twice, three years ago. It's a disturbing mix, I'll admit.

'Now stretch your hands up, right up, and go on to your toes. That's it! Now, drop that and… lunge. Big lunge. Feel your bum and core getting a good stretch.'

There's a giggle at the back from Bethany.

'Now Bluebells, do you all remember the steps? I'm not looking at anyone. Gurpreet, darling, I'm not looking at you.'

'Oh oh oh, Miss!' Gurpreet waves her arms wildly like she's got all the answers to the SATs tucked into her knickers. 'I found a new remembering trick, see?' There's a little green leaf tucked into her left shoelaces. 'When you leave somewhere, you have left. See? So the leaf means left!'

I squeeze her shoulder. 'Genius! Latin ballroom, here you come. Now, girls, it's ten to, so we're going to walk in a nice orderly line over to the arena to wait for the announcer to say we're going to dance. Then the music will start and I'll give the sign to start.'

Veronica has her arms behind her back at the front of the group. 'And what is the sign to start?'

'I'll say "start".' She rolls her eyes. The only eight-year-old I know who has no time for silliness. She's probably silently working out a Middle Eastern peace agreement while I'm bleating on about securely tied shoelaces and smiling to the crowd.

I lead the girls away from the grass behind our tent to the arena. I'm so glad we have warmed up because what's before me is a perfect *West Side Story* moment: Alex, with his gang of mini uniformed idiots, and me with my prancing Bluebells.

'Girls, take your places. I'll be right back after I've had a word with The Su— the Scout Master.'

'Ooooooh!' say all the Bluebells, bar Veronica.

I see Alex point his troupe in the same direction. They're on after us with some lame camp building demonstration. Yawn. Give me chirpy country music and a gigantic pole any day. He's coming my way. In his pressed uniform. Damn. I so wanted to storm up to him, to look as intimidating as I can muster.

'Mistress Bloom.' Sarky git.

'Scout Master. How are you?'

'Very we—'

'Yes, actually, what I wanted to say to you, is please stop filling the young minds of this village with tosh.'

'Sorry?' He shoves his hands in his khaki shorts. They are ridiculous. And make me very happy. Even his toned legs poking out the bottom can't distract from how stupid little boy shorts are on a grown man.

I lace my fingers together. 'You've told the Scouts that the Hall is going to be torn down. That remains to be seen, doesn't it? And I might add: over my dead body. So keep your nonsense to yourself and keep busy with dib dibs and getting to sleep at night knowing you professionally sell off beloved landmarks. Because you really should know that we—'

My Hillary-Clinton-worthy rant is interrupted by a tug at my t-shirt and a tearful Veronica. 'The boys…' she hiccups, 'they're being so mean.'

'What are they doing, love?'

'They saying we're… we're pole dancers… and strippers!'

'WHAT!' I bellow, spinning on my heels. I can see two Scouts faux-twerking in front of a group of sobbing Bluebells. The rest of the boys are laughing and jeering, bar a few pale-faced conscientious objectors at the back. But before I can do my best Storm from *X-Men* impression and rain some fury down on these little arses, Alex has beaten me to it and is striding off at a lightning speed. Maybe to get in first and get their stories straight. Typical.

I jog after him and flinch when he starts shouting. 'Fall in line! Never, ever have I heard of such atrocious behaviour. Unacceptable! Utterly unacceptable! You have shown yourselves up, Scouts. You have been rude, discourteous and… I'm so disappointed. That's it – I'm cancelling our display.'

The faint mewls of protest are met with a glare from Alex. Wow, when he goes for it, he goes for it. I wouldn't like to take the last Kit Kat in his snack drawer.

I'm still mid-storm, so I end up standing just behind him. 'And what would you like to add, Mistress Bloom?'

'Oh. Only that I agree completely with you, Scout Master. I've never seen anything like it in nearly 30 years of living in Hazlehurst. I'm appalled. And I'll certainly be talking to Mrs Simmons at your school about it.' I don't care that I sound like someone's maiden aunt, I am not letting these little misogynists in the making get away without a lesson in respect.

'Now you can all go and find your parents and explain just why they won't be watching you erect a tent at twelve thirty. GO!' he yells, when they keep standing, dumbstruck.

With this fourteen young pups disperse, tails dragging behind them.

'I'm sorry, ladies.' Alex addresses my troupe. 'It shouldn't have happened and it certainly won't happen again. Don't suppose you could use any help today, could you? Someone to bring you orange slices at half time?'

The girls laugh, their tears and tensions slowly slipping away. Veronica wipes the back of her hand under her eyes. 'It doesn't work like that. We just keep going. But you could press play on the tape deck, thank you.'

Alex salutes her. 'It would be an honour to serve the mighty Bluebells.'

'Right, OK, girls. Time to go. Everyone look for your families, give them a big smile. If you forget what to do, yell at Veronica. But you won't, because you'll be fine!'

My girls really pull it out of the bag, considering the drama they've endured just minutes before doing their do si dos and backwards turns. Gurpreet is picture-perfect, even managing to wave at her mum and dad without letting go of her ribbon. As the last wheeze of the music crackles through the speakers, we have a beautiful woven pattern down the pole and the audience of villagers break out into loud, spontaneous applause. What more could you want from your average maypole dance?

I'm beaming with pride as the girls file out neatly and Alex returns with the boom box.

'Impressive.' He nods. 'And I am sorry about before. I've got a few hard nuts, with some problems, and they lead the others astray. But they're going to find next week's meeting about feminism really instructive.'

I splutter out a laugh. I can't help it.

'What?'

'You're going to do feminism? With the Scouts?'

'Yes.' Alex blinks and shrinks back a little, like I'd just pinched him somewhere soft. 'Why, is that weird? It's not just women that can be feminists, you know.' I'm about to muster a reply to say that Of course I know men can be feminists, thank you very much, capitalist swine, when he adjusts his toggle and looks edgy. 'Ah, one of the hard nut dads is looking for me, I can see. This will be fun. I'll swing by the tent later, say hello. It looks really impressive.'

And at that I am truly gobsmacked into silence. He's impressed? With me? And my attempts to derail him?

Eh?

Lucy, Steve and I are taking a super speedy sandwich break. Well, it's not so much a break as standing a few paces away from the action and shoving panini down our necks. There is a frenzy of colouring in going on at our bunting crafts table. Steve took a free Mindfulness Colouring sheet the school was sent and photocopied it in a triangle shape. So now the local kids, and a few stressed-looking grown ups, are getting busy with the crayons to colour and create their own bunting. Susannah is currently supervising the stapling of each bit onto the string, but when I've polished off this ham and cheese toastie I'll relieve her. She's been grafting today.

We're serenaded by my little choir singing 'White Cliffs of Dover' and it's probably one of the most bonkers moments of my life. As I see a mum and her two boys finish their scribbling and get up to leave, I thrust a leaflet at her with greasy paws. 'Funday Monday, come and join us at the Hall!' I hope I communicated some energy and happiness through my gobful of lunch.

'Nice work,' Lucy says as she wipes her mouth and chucks her paper plate in the bin. 'God, there's such a great vibe today. I think we're going to do this!' She gives an air punch and Stevie shakes his head in joyful embarrassment.

'It has all gone swimmingly, apart from The Suit exploding in the middle of the field. Super weird. What was that about?' Steve turns to me.

'Oh, some Scouts being little nob— um, ne'er-do-wells.' Abel rushes past my legs, flapping two bunting triangles like pterodactyl wings and squawking. 'He was actually pretty good about putting them right.'

Steve's eyebrows do a little dance. 'Really? Maybe he's teacher material.'

'No.' Lucy shakes her head. 'Looking at that fancy suit he wears, he's far too attached to material luxuries and any kind of comfort. He's all about the money.' She elbows me. 'So when you were chatting to him after, were you giving him what for about the Hall? Oooh, wish I could have listened in. I missed *East-Enders* last night too.'

I fold my paper plate in half and then quarters, fiddling with the crease. 'No, actually. We were talking about feminism. And he said our tent was 'impressive'. So… Yeah.'

'Blimey. Unexpected.'

'You're telling me.'

Luce sticks her finger in the air. 'We should be extra careful. It might be a let-our-guard-down thing. He might be plotting some kind of, some kind of sabotage.'

Steve pulls her in toward him by her waist. 'Love, you definitely missed *EastEnders* last night. I doubt it'll come down to the Scout Master at the local fete with the candlestick. I mean, he might be a fat cat, but he can't be entirely evil. He's a feminist, it seems.'

—

The fete, as usual, does not disappoint. It's so packed full of country charm that it's like someone very timid has edited an episode of *Midsommer Murders* and taken out all the grisly bits. The WI have not only produced enough scones to keep a warship afloat for six months, but they've also been crazy busy with their knitting needles to make little teddies and dollies to run a tombola for a local children's hospice. I see one lime green and purple striped teddy. I'm guessing it came from Flip's craft stash.

I waste all my loose change on the coconut shy until the man running it takes mercy on me and gives me a massive bottle of dandelion and burdock. But it's my prize and I'm happy with it. I'm lugging it to the chairs around the central arena to bag two seats for the dog show – Mum is meeting me here. I have five hot doughnuts in my pocket and at least two of them have her name on. We've watched this dog show together for as long as I can remember and we always root for the unruly, ugly one no one else is cheering for. We like the underdog… dog. Heck, we are the underdog dogs at the moment.

I'm settled on a stool, my litre of undrinkable stuff looking menacing on the chair next to me. No one is daring to ask if it's free. If I ever go on a big city night out again, I'm putting dandelion and burdock in my bag for the night train home. Just as I take a bite out of an impossibly fluffy doughnut, my phone rattles in my pocket.

Mum: *Not feeling bright. Heading to bed. Sorry, pet.*

Oh. A lone underdog today, then. I sniff and slide the phone back into my jeans. Still, now I don't need to explain the missing doughnuts, I suppose.

I think dog number four is my favourite this year: a Jack Russell called Terry with three legs and an unattractive lolling tongue. Terry, it's you and me versus the world.

'Go Terry!' I yell, warm sugar dusting my legs as I cheer him on through the assault course. Weaving around those little sticks is no laughing matter when you can hardly stand upright. He's a tripod, for goodness sake. But I believe in him!

Three doughnuts and impassioned dog cheerleading can make a lady quite thirsty. I'm tilting the big plastic bottle of dark fizzy stuff to my lips just as there's a gentle 'Ahem' behind me. It's Flip with a hot looking guy in grey chinos and a lumberjack shirt.

'Hey Connie! This is Marcus, from the *Mirror*.'

Oh. I'd been expecting a woman with a tidy little suit and a big hairdo, for some reason. Someone who could have been an estate agent or an Avon lady just as much as a journalist writing human-interest pieces for a red top. Not a gorgeous hipster type. And he's probably only about twenty-five.

I'm suddenly painfully away of the crispy sugar forming a crust around my lips and try to delicately bat it away with the heel of my hand. 'Hi! Lovely to meet you!' I shoot up from my stool and grab his hand.

'And you. Sorry, are we disturbing you?' He nods towards the arena, where the contestants are making their final walk around the space.

'Not at all. Just supporting the local community! It's what I'm all about!' I wince as I actually hear the exclamation points boom out through my voice.

'He hasn't started the interview yet,' Flip whispers in my direction. 'Pace yourself.'

Marcus snaps a few pictures on his iPhone. It's one of those big ones that you can hardly fit in your hand. That's how hipster he is. 'This is great. Great dogs. And look at that little guy!' He points out Terry, not taking his place in the line-up and swaying slightly in the breeze.

'He's my favourite, actually! Terry the three-legged wonder.'

One of the judges bends down to our man and puts a yellow ribbon on his collar.

'Has he won!?' Marcus keeps snapping away.

Something about how this journo is taking Terry to his heart really warms my cockles. 'He's won the special commendation, which is a big deal even if it isn't technically best in show.'

Marcus smiles, and it's one of those mega fill-your-face smiles. 'Brilliant. Go Terry!'

'Exactly!'

Flip points her finger between us. 'Well now you two dog lovers are acquainted, I'm going to get back to my PR duties, fight the good fight. Marcus, thanks for coming out. Connie here will give you the whole story, I'm sure.'

As she speed-walks off behind Marcus, she gives me a big double thumbs up, with a tongue waggle for good measure. 'Super hot!' she mouths, with a pervy eye roll.

I give the tiniest nod to acknowledge I've seen her and I agree, or she could go on like that for a while. Yes. He is super hot. Almost unnervingly hot.

'So tell me a bit about your bunting campaign. Start at the beginning and just keep going.' Marcus sits down on a plastic chair and taps something on his phone – must be a recording app.

I'm suddenly very aware of my limbs as I try and sit smoothly back down on my stool. But I've crossed my legs in a blokey kind of way and now I'm too flustered to rearrange myself. Damn.

'Yes. Well, it all starts with my Gran, actually. Rosemarie Duncan. She was the caretaker of Bluebell Hall for forty years and when she died the job sort of passed to me. And now,' my eyes flick up to the tent, a way off in the distance but just over Marcus's shoulder in my eyeline. It's an explosion of colour and activity, even from over here. But an incongruous figure stands outside, legs planted far apart, arms crossed, ridiculous shorts flapping in the spring breeze. Alex. He's staring right at me.

He must have twigged we've got some serious media interest and he's fuming. I want to laugh, just as I also feel a weird flutter in my stomach.

'Now?' Marcus prompts.

'And now it's under threat. From a big corporation. So in Hazlehurst we're coming together as a community to save it. And you've come just in the nick of time.'

I give what I hope is my most confident and winning smile and lean in even closer to dish my story. Hopefully by Bank Holiday morning everyone is going to know it too.

–

I am truly pooped. I can barely lift my arm to wave off Marcus's taxi. He tried to book an Uber to take him back to London but I had to tell him we didn't get the big city stuff round here. So Hazlehurst Happy Motors it is.

Giving good soundbites is surprisingly exhausting. Marcus and I chatted for over two hours as the fete played out around us – the vintage car show rumbled into the arena and tooted a selection of old horns, the Medieval re-enactment society did a very long and slow dance wearing 'authentic' sweaty nylon robes and every ten minutes or so I would peek over to where Steve, Luce, Susannah and Flip were busy thrusting leaflets at locals, crafting up bunting with kids and even starting up a chant of 'Hell, no, we won't go!' until the local reverend came over with a bit of a cross look on his face.

I slope back towards my hardworking comrades and am rewarded with a cup of tea from Susannah's flask and a big hug from my fill-in gran. 'She would have been so proud,' she says into my ear. And we both know who she means.

'So so so?!' Flip dances round me, her bracelets clanking on her arms.

I rub my hands over my face and try and smooth my bob back into some sort of shape. 'I think that went well. I think I said what we needed to say. I put the call out for more visitors in no uncertain terms. So now to cross our fingers and wait for the paper, I guess...'

Susannah and Flip exchange a now well-rehearsed fist bump and Luce squeezes Steve's hands. Today the fete has been ours. It has been perfect.

'Rain!' yells Abel as he ducks under our awning and runs between his dad's legs. 'Rain, rain, go away, you're on my head and I can't play!'

Sure enough, there's a fine mist of rain now coming down. That kind of rain that doesn't look like much but the air is so full of it you're soaked in seconds.

'Well, you can't have it all,' Susannah says, as ever my Yoda.

More and more villagers are taking refuge in our big tent, grabbing pencils and joining in the bunting colouring or nosing at our history displays. Susannah sent the choir home a while back, when they were starting to nod off in their deckchairs.

Flip pulls me to her side. 'Did you get his number?'

'Oh god, did you need me to? I thought you would have had it already.'

She gives an eye roll so exasperated that I worry it's going to compromise her jade green eyeliner. 'No, for you. Did YOU get his number, for yourself?'

Half of the Scout troop rush in, with their annoying leader, and now there's very little breathing space in here, let alone a quiet corner to discuss hot menfolk.

'Um, I didn't think of it like that. I was just thinking of him as a journalist. For the campaign.'

'But could you think of him as a man, for the bedroom?' Flip bites down on her bottom lip.

'Ssshhhhh!'

'Yes, if you wouldn't mind keeping it down,' Alex grumbles. 'I am trying to teach my scouts not to think of people as sex objects, so it would be great if you could do the same.'

'Pah!' Flip shrugs, not even turning around to acknowledge him.

'And can I just say as a professional that it's hardly... fitting to talk about someone like that when they're just doing their job. It's not professional in itself.'

I'm a bit lost for a good rebuttal. I think he might have us on this one. But Flip just gives a killer Beyoncé 'Boy, bye' hand flick. 'I don't think someone who professionally crushes dreams should give out job advice, 'kay?'

Uh oh. Flip can't see but I can – he's now pushing his way determinedly through the throng of people to reach our corner.

He takes a deep breath and pushes up his sleeves. 'Can we just get this straight? Can we, please? My job is not to crush dreams, I'm not a fat cat, I'm not a corporate robot. I advise trusts on how best to manage their assets, for the longevity of their operation. I help them, and so I help the people they employ and the people they serve. There. That's it. I'm not a Marvel villain. I'm a man.' He lets out a long sigh, a full lung's worth. 'I'm doing my job and I'm trying to be a part of this village.'

Flip's mouth hangs a little way open. I think our professional talker is lost for words.

'Scouts,' he calls over his shoulder, 'we're off. A little rain never hurt anyone. Even corporate robots can take a bit of drizzle.'

'Blimey,' Flip says eventually, as the boys march off. 'Knickers in a twist, or what?' So Alex may not be a dream-crusher but he's still got a way to go in being a persuasive public speaker, then.

Steve squeezes his way over to us. 'I think this might be wind down time, guys. The Committee seem to think this rain isn't going to clear up for a few hours and it's 3.25 p.m., so we've had the best of the day. Still a big victory for Bluebell Hall!' He shoulder barges me and the knots I've been carrying around between my shoulder blades are knocked away. I can relax for the first time in ages – people now know about us and they want to be part of it. We've had so many passionate promises of help and support today, loads of people saying they'd be coming on Monday, that we might just reach of capacity for Monday Funday! That would be a great postscript to the story, maybe another little piece for Marcus. *Local Hall Saved – Villagers Unite! A Community Tied Together By Bunting!* I can already hear the happy squawks of kids racing about on the parquet, the happy chatter of parents as they enjoy a cup of tea and admire the new colour scheme, the log book growing fat and stuffed with signatures. Bluebell Hall is going back to its roots: it's going to bring everyone together.

The rain looks like it's getting fatter and definitely settling in for a bit of a spring soaking. 'Come on guys, the iced buns are on me.'

Chapter 14

I really couldn't sleep last night: whether it was the big dreams I had in mind for Monday Funday (with the numbers I estimated, a conga line was just too good to resist), or imagining how the newspaper write-up would go, or maybe it was just the drum of raindrops on the roof but I tossed and turned in my spotty duvet cover until about five a.m., when I decided a run would sort me out.

Now I'm pounding along the Hazlehurst streets while everyone else is still rightly tucked up in bed this early on a Sunday. Just a few flickering street lights to keep me company, that and the drizzle that hasn't really stopped since yesterday afternoon. I haven't been for a run for so long – I used to be really keen about it when I lived in Manchester. I'd go out three or four times a week, running around the quayside, startling the first commuters into spilling their cappuccinos. It would always set me up for the day ahead, even if it was just a day of mindless spreadsheet filling. I suppose round here there are too many former A-level crushes living nearby that might just spot me in my bobbly leggings and my ungainly bouncing boobs. That kind of worry stops it being so feel-good.

But this morning I doubt I'll bump into Kevin Morgan at 5.47 a.m. on the footpath around the local farm. Not unless he has some really dodgy habits he's hiding. I'm making up a running route as I go along, following the funny little 'blue plates' of historical interest that the Village Committee put up when I was a teenager. Places of interest… to anyone born and bred in Hazlehurst, I'd say. Here's Hibbert Park, set up by our generous benefactor because apparently he was quite fond of watching a speckle-breasted thrush and wanted to preserve them in the village. Next I'm whizzing past the Post Office, once the site of the village's poorhouse and jail. Still sometimes a place for drawn-out suffering, if you ask me. And now round Jenny's Corner: the corner at which the very first woman to ride a bicycle in Hazlehurst clambered on her brother's bike, tucked her skirts up between her knees and wobbled off down the road. Rather shocking at the time, apparently – it left her ankles in plain view. By the swings and slides on the common is a blue plaque that reminds us this wasn't always just a space for teenagers to come and eat chips on the roundabout, but back at the time of the Domesday Book it was an area for people to graze their animals and keep themselves and their families fed. That's why, every year since then, the May Day fete has been held on the common to celebrate surviving the winter and embracing the summer to come. We just now happen to throw in a bouncy castle and afternoon tea for good measure.

The endorphins pumping through my system are perfectly drowning out all the thoughts and to-dos and what-ifs that shouted at me all night. It's just me and my battered Asics and together we're disappearing into fields and lanes and cut-throughs… Except that I've brought myself to the back of the Hall. So much for switching off. My subconscious has clearly done my laces up this morning and taken charge of the map reading on this little adventure. Right. Well, if I can't get around my jumpy mind with a run, I'll just have to get started on everything that needs doing. And luckily a broom doesn't mind if you've only got your grubby running kit on. I want this place spick and span for all its new visitors tomorrow. If we're going to turn them into regulars they need to fall in love with the Hall on sight.

But as I near the front door, I see something that breaks my heart into tiny, sharp pieces. There's water running out from under the door. Oh cripes, not the loos again!

I open the heavy door in a hurry, taking big squelchy steps towards the bathroom. Damn these breathable trainers – absorbing every bit of old toilet water they can.

But there's no eruption of water coming from the toilets themselves – or the sinks. What the what? I dash into the kitchen to check the sink there. And that's when it hits me. The pigeon.

It flaps directly into my face with a wonky lunge, disturbed by my panicked sprinting, probably, and after a flustered flight around the kitchen cupboards, it disappears into the sky. Because I can see the sky. Through the big hole in the ceiling. So this is where the water is from: last night's persistent rainfall. It must have been the final straw for the roof and now we have a skylight which is definitely not adding value.

Crumbly flakes of plaster and wood float about my ankles. And I'm crying.

—

God bless Luce, even at this and hour on a Sunday, she's here ten minutes after I call her. Her North Face jacket is slung over tartan pjs and there are still smudges of yesterday's mascara under her eyes. But when she heard my bleats down the phone, she didn't hesitate.

'Oh no.' I was hoping she would tell me it wasn't as bad as it looked, in her professional opinion as a quantity surveyor. Just a case of some new timbers, tidying up and a new emulsion. But she's shaking her head very slowly, over and over. 'Oh Connie. I'm so sorry. This is… this is very serious. I don't actually like us standing here. Let's move outside.'

I wade after her, wishing I'd asked her to bring a pair of wellies for me, too. My feet are seriously feeling the bite of cold water. But the sinking realisation of what is coming next hurts more.

Luce studies the toes of her blue flowery boots on the gravel outside. 'You need to close up, call the estate. Connie, no one can go in there.'

'I know.' My voice is scratchy and wobbly all at once.

'Not even you, OK?'

'OK.'

'I really mean it. If the roof went after moderate rain, even if it has been persistent, then there's something very wrong here. And it's not fit for visitors.'

I can hardly swallow. 'Yes.'

She pulls me into the biggest bear hug her small frame can muster. 'Oh, love. What unbelievably shitty timing.'

'Language, Mum.'

'There's no Abel here, and this situation really calls for it. Will you be able to get hold of someone from the estate on a Sunday? I just think, for public safety, we should get it properly shut up. Signs posted and that kind of stuff.'

I roll my eyes, and that's all she needs to see to work it out.

'The Suit. Shitty shit.'

I blow out a big, slow breath and dig my nails into my palms to stop myself crying. It's an old trick from when I was little and Mum wasn't well. 'Hope his favourite Ted Baker also comes in a waterproof number. Ugh, this is all his Christmasses come at once.'

Luce wipes under her eyes. 'Let's not think about him now. First things first, we switch off the power, water and gas. Anything you need to save from inside? It might be your last chance for a good while.'

But before she's finished her sentence I'm already bolting for the door, barging it open and lunging for two things that mean the world to me right now: the log book, curling at the edges from the damp, and the framed picture of Gran that sits beside it. I press the picture against my chest. 'Don't look, Gran. Just don't look.'

I can't bear the thought of having to see Alex right now, so I dig his number out of one of the letters he's sent that I tucked into the log book, and send a message to his mobile. I leave the key in a pot by the front door, and seeing that Alex has received the text and is writing a reply, I quickly switch off my phone and start the walk home. Luce offers me a lift, but I really need some thinking time.

I pass the park, where volunteer litter pickers have turned up unbearably early to spruce the place up after yesterday's fete.

I sprint over the damp grass to where I can see Brian. I ignore the protests of my wet and cold feet. They can suck it up. 'Need any more help?'

'Connie! How wonderful! Yes, we do. Doris over there has the sticks. Thank you so much. You know, I'm sending my letter to the Hibbert estate first thing on Tuesday, telling them how I see the Hall as an integral part of this village. And you, too, young lady. You have done something of real worth.'

I sling a black bag over my shoulder and dig my nails into my palms again. 'Yes… Well.' I'm too weary to talk. He'll hear soon enough. They all will.

After about an hour of stabbing empty Fanta cans and chip papers, letting my frustrations go into every movement of my litter stick, I have just about enough energy left to call in at the corner shop, pick up a massive bar of Cadbury's and some Wotsits and wearily plod home.

Mum's on the sofa, in her pjs, when I get in. Her skin is grey and tears have left shining tracks on her cheeks. 'Oh, darling,' she murmurs as I fall into her arms. 'What a thing to happen. I'm so sorry.'

I don't know if there's an acceptable time limit to sobbing into your mum's hair when you are almost 30, but I certainly pass it. I just can't seem to stop, even though I know it won't change anything. She squeezes me tightly around my middle.

'At least Gran wasn't here to see it. That's the only bright side I can think of.'

But it's stupid of me to bring Gran into it, because Mum's eyes get watery again. I unload my snack haul onto the coffee table as if that's going to magically turn back time. But we both just stare at the calories and saturated fats and bright orange flavourings like a pair of Slimming World zealots. It's one of the rare moments of my life when I can't blink at a bar of Dairy Milk and have it disappear. All the restless energy of first thing this morning has deserted me and I am instead full of inertia. Like my limbs and my head and my stomach are all full of rocks and I can't move, can't think, can't even start to put together a plan to improve things. It just makes me tired, the magnitude of it all.

The roof is gone. We don't have the money to fix it, and we certainly don't have the skills to attempt a bodge job ourselves. I don't think Luce would let me, anyway, out of professional honour. The floors will be ruined from the flooding. The new paint work, too. It will probably need rewiring, plastering too, and in all of that all the other health and safety violations will probably come to light. Even if I had time, I'm not sure I could ever raise that kind of money. People are generous here but persuading them to give up much needed cash for a disused pile of soggy timbers might even be beyond the powers of the Bunting Society.

The Hall has given up on me, just as we were really kicking butt. Just as it was about to be the new second home to so many people, it's left us homeless. It's left me jobless. What will I do now? Join Mum down at Budgens? Sell hundreds of meters of nearly new bunting at a car boot sale? And without my mission to save the Hall keeping me busy and focused, I can hardly ignore that I have no life plan. I hardly have what you'd call a life. I can't imagine my life without the Hall – the choir, the families, the Bluebells.

Oh, the Bluebells. They really will have to get along with the Scouts now, if we want to keep the group going. Veronica is going to come out in hives. I might too, having to be at close quarters with Alex week in, week out. And hear him describe the Hall's transition into a brand soaking new mega Costa, I bet. He might make out he's not the fat cat bad guy, but now the Hall is his to do with as he pleases. So we'll soon see what he's really made of.

The palms of my hands are starting to look like I've been at them with a cheese grater now, but I can't cry any more in front of Mum. Just when I thought she was starting to have a really long good spell, this is exactly the kind of thing that can turn a rocky patch into a major low. Losing the Hall and all our family history that's linked to it is like losing a small piece of Gran all over again. When we were there, we were close to her, in a weird way. And now the next time we're there we'll probably be ordering grande mocha chai tea coolers, and that would have really got Gran's goat, in more ways than one.

The last four years of my life have collapsed into a puddle on a ruined kitchen floor, without even anyone to see it, or wave it goodbye. Bar a fat, flapping pigeon. Just a damp disappointment. A really bad end to a great weekend. I feel like I've just come home from Glastonbury to be told the world is going to end a week on Tuesday.

Mum and I sit motionless on the sofa for a few hours, not quite awake and not quite asleep, ignoring the junk food and the phone when it rings and later a soft knock at the door.

Because, really, what's the point now?

Chapter 15

Hunger woke me up in the end. And a stiff neck from being slumped against Mum's shoulder all afternoon.

Neither of us really know what we want to eat, so we're going through the motions with a takeaway from the chippy. If in doubt, fall back on fried potato.

My phone's still off, and I unplugged the landline on my way out the door – its shrill ring was biting on my last nerve. There's hardly anything urgent to worry about now. The Hall is Alex's problem. Just the way he wanted it.

But I like being without a phone, which is not something I would have predicted after a whole day off Facebook and email and the *Daily Mail* sidebar of shame. I don't need to be on top of it all. The world is turning without me. It's going to do its own thing. I'm going to do mine. With a side of mushy peas.

I'm in a slow daydream about living in a wood cabin and eating foraged mushrooms for the rest of my adult life, when the jangle of the shop door brings me back to reality. No, I couldn't live like that. I'd miss the chippy too much.

'Connie!' Dom's strong grip spins me around. 'At last! We've been ringing and ringing. Susannah went round to see you. We've all been so worried.'

I shrug. 'The Hall is done with, sorry Dom. Worrying won't bring it back. It's… It's a gonner. Sorry.'

His bushy eyebrows bunch together. 'We've been worried about you. Luce told us all and we wanted to see how you were, but no one could track you down. You do a better job of vanishing off the grid than my Polly.'

'Oh. Right. Sorry. How is Polly? I didn't see her yesterday.' There's a twist in my stomach as I picture our tent at the fete, full of smiles and crossed fingers and bright hopes. Suddenly I don't think I will be able to do much with my medium haddock and chips.

Dom shoves his hands in his pockets. 'She was meant to help out. But she didn't. Said she was with friends, but wouldn't tell me who. Came back late smelling of some strange perfume. Not that she has money to buy some so where that's come from… But I'm not boring you with that today. We're having an emergency meeting, at Flip's house.'

'I don't follow you.'

'Well, we've got to make a plan. About our next steps. For the Hall.'

Now the twisting feeling is sitting behind my eyes, aching and itching in my brain. 'There's no plan, Dom. It's done. The Hall is a wreck, we can't invite people to a health hazard. There's no time left and so we're done.' I rub the arm of his bomber jacket. 'But we tried. We gave it our best.'

The tired-looking lady behind the counter pushes a big, warm paper parcel in my direction.

'I've got to go, get back to Mum.'

'So that's it? You're walking away?'

I feel stung by the edge to his voice. 'Look, I don't have a million quid or *DIY SOS* up my sleeve. We did all that was realistically possible and it was great, while it lasted. But this is out of my hands. It's out of all of our hands. I appreciate that you guys want to give it another shot but... I think this is it.'

Dom's open mouth snaps into a firm line as I take my food and let the door bell jangle behind me.

Stevie is filling our little sofa with his stocky frame when I get home.

'Thank god you're here, you can help us with this order. I went nuts and got two battered sausages that we're just never going to eat. Oh, where's Mum?'

Steve sits up a little against the limp sofa cushions. 'She wanted a lie-down. I told her I'd hang around for you. I think she's worried about you, Cons.'

I press a can of Pepsi against my forehead. The cold switches off the twisty feeling for a moment. 'Well that makes for a neat circle of worry. Because I think she's having a… wobble again.'

I unwrap the fish and chips, and get some plates. Stevie picks up a battered sausage and nibbles at it. 'I don't even know why I'm eating this. I've had a full-on lamb roast at home.'

'You've eaten greasy food on that sofa since you wore skater shoes and beaded chokers, and don't you forget it. Anyway, you're doing me a favour because I've pretty much lost my appetite. I doubt Mum will come back down again tonight, a reheated fish and chips is the devil's food.'

He points the sausage at me. 'Eat. If I go home and tell Luce you didn't look after yourself under my watch, I'll be in for it. She'll confiscate my favourite highlighters.'

I wave the sausage away. 'Shut up, I'm fine. Just had a long day.'

Steve rolls his eyes. 'You did a runner and switched your phone off. You and your mum went full-on hermit. Sounds like Susannah nearly pounded the door down, to no reply. So she was on the blower to Luce; Dom and Flip were deployed for a street by street search. And I had Alex on my doorstep.' He says the last bit like a casual aside but there's nothing casual about my reaction.

'WHAT!?'

'He said he wanted to follow up with you, but you'd gone dark. I mean, he actually said 'gone dark'. Think the poor guys stays in alone too much with his *Bourne* DVDs.'

'Why did he go to you? How did he even know where you lived!? That's bloody creepy.'

'Yes, that's what I thought at first.' Steve chews on a fat chip. 'But apparently I'm your emergency contact on your employment documents, so that's where he got it from.' He clutches his heart in mock-drama. 'I'm so touched that you want me there when you break an ankle mopping the floor, or stab yourself with a needle on a bunting mission.'

I whip his plate off his lap and he pouts. 'Hardly counts anymore, now I'm unemployed. Nob. Thanks for rubbing it in.' I chew on the end of the drawstring of my hoodie. 'I can't believe he came to your house.'

'I think Luce enjoyed the chance to study him at close quarters. But, you know, after a chat, I kind of,' Stevie fiddles with the curls at the nape of his neck, 'ah, I kind of think maybe he's not as evil as we previously thought.'

The crispy batter really scratches my throat as I almost choke to death.

'Wait, wait, wait. Before you go for me and Abel is denied a sibling, just listen. He's a decent bloke. He's been round to the Hall, done all the health and safety malarkey at breakneck speed, even sat down with Luce for her professional opinion and took all sort of notes. He's roused all the board members on a Sunday to keep them up to speed. And amongst all that, he went to his office, found an address for you and tracked me down. He wanted to check you were OK.' Stevie can see I'm hurrying to wash my mouthful down with a drink so he rushes on. 'I know you want different things for the Hall, but he's not really a big bad wolf. Not when you listen to him about his job, beyond wearing a fancy suit and pissing you off.'

'Ergh.'

'And, in your duty as a pillar of the community, you should really be nicer to new people in the village. He's doing his job, volunteering with the Scouts; I think he really wants to fit in here. I mean, I don't exactly want to hang out at the pub with most of the parents from my class, but it is my duty to be nice to them.'

I slowly bite a chip dipped in peas.

'Though, if you did want to have a drink with him…'

'Steve! Seriously?'

He holds his arms up. 'It's been a while since you had a gentleman caller. No one, in fact, since that pillock in Manchester. You're seeing his posh suit as a bad thing – maybe it's a sign he has a good, reliable income. He could be a catch! Or maybe someone to just polish up your skills on.' He says this last bit almost under his breath. I'd love to come zinging back with a reply that my dating skills are laser sharp, thanks very much, but my confidence wibbles out on me.

'Look, I'd better get back. I've left Luce to do bedtime and, much as I love her, she's frankly rubbish at the Gruffalo's voice.' Steve pulls his arms through his jacket and heads for the door. 'Don't enjoy the misery for too long, eh? I know you might be done with the Hall now, but the other guys are finding it hard to let go. They need to see you. Even if it's not to whip up a thousand more metres of protest bunting, they're still your mates. Don't forget that. And give my love to your mum.' He closes the front door gently behind him.

–

I haven't found the energy to switch my phone back on after a rubbish night's sleep but I have found the guts to go and visit my little choir with some thank you gifts for their sterling performance at the fete. They don't have to know our plans have all been washed down the drain together with a rotten roof joist; I'm not sure how it would help anyone to fill them in. So I'm loaded down with Werther's, daffodils and some custard creams to perk them up. Steve's comment yesterday about enjoying my misery hit exactly the mark he meant it to. I might have lost my job, lost my moral crusade, but I still have people I'm responsible for.

After I've poured a lot of tea and reassured Delilah that, yes, I really will hurry up and get married before I end up a right old maid, I knock on Susannah's door.

When she sees me on her welcome mat, she folds her arms and cocks her hip. A sassy but risky move when you're no spring chicken. 'And so here you are. At last.'

My smile is so sheepish I can feel fleece growing out of my ears. 'Sorry. I needed a bit of time… To process.'

With a huff she lets me in. 'That Oprah speak is all well and good but you could have at least told us yourself, before you did your big vanishing act. It was all such a shock and then we had no Connie, to boot. It not what—'

'Not what Gran would have done. I know. I'm sorry.'

'Actually, I was going to say it's not what leaders do. Believe it or not, your gran isn't the benchmark for all situations, my dear. She wouldn't have got this far, in my humble opinion.'

I sit down with an 'oof' on one of Susannah's neat armchairs. 'What do you mean?'

She waves her hands. 'Talking to the media, setting up the stall at the fete to really make a noise. I don't doubt she would have been bending some ears about the closure, oh yes. But I don't think she would have been able to think so big, not like you did.' She spots my frown. 'That's not a criticism, that's just putting things in context. She was raised in a very different era. That woman had backbone and gumption, but her world was smaller than yours. Her world was this village, and she wouldn't have been able to see beyond the status quo. But you did. You saw big things for the Hall.' She sits down across from me. 'Even if you don't see them for yourself.'

'You're not going to join Delilah's gang and badger me up the aisle, are you?'

Susannah rolls her eyes. 'Men are never a priority. But your career should be. Your Gran devoted herself to this place because there were no boardroom doors open for her, no masters degrees, no departure lounges waiting. In your shoes, who knows where she would have ended up. Probably giving Alan Sugar a run for his money, no doubt.' She leans forward and pats my knees gently. 'I'm so happy you came back to be with your mum but I didn't think four years later you'd still be here, love. And the way you reacted to the leak—'

'It's a bit more than that! The roof caved in!'

Susannah nods. 'It did. And it's awful. But the way you reacted... it made me think that perhaps it's not healthy to have just one thing in your life. Even if you truly love it. We can treasure those important things, but it shouldn't stop us looking for more, for new passions.'

I get up and rub away invisible crumbs from my lap, to avoid her eyes. 'Yes, well... it's been on my mind recently. Where I'd go, beyond the Hall. And now I guess I don't have any choice but to find the answer. As rubbish as it feels.'

Susannah lets out a long sigh. 'Your Gran was my best friend. I miss her everyday. She loved you so ferociously. She wanted you to have the best in life, and she wanted you to live it to the full. I'm not sure being tied like this to the village, teaching girls to maypole, visiting old folks with your time off, I'm not sure that's what she would have pictured.'

And I know she's right. And this feels so much worse than the roof.

After quickly clearing my throat, I move straight back towards the door. 'Disappointing Gran was the last thing I ever wanted. Must get going. Bye.'

Chapter 16

I've always found that by hanging out with kids that you somehow, magically, borrow a bit of their energy and enthusiasm. Sort of like the film *Cocoon*, but not so creepy and with fewer perms.

An evening with the Bluebells and I'm usually whistling some little Bieber tune and jigging about as I'm stacking chairs and throwing away Mini Cheddars packets at the end of the night. But I'm making my way to the first Bluebell meeting ever to be held outside of Bluebell Hall like my trainers are full of lead and my horoscope just read 'DOOM' this morning. It's been a shower of a week, a very bad cover of the Craig David classic: discovered the Hall was a wreck on Sunday, felt like a loser on Monday, futile job searches on Tuesday, and now I'm at a Scout hut and very much not about to chill with the person there.

As I push open the stiff door to the Scout hut, a small and modern affair tucked behind the high street, I take a deep breath.

'When they go low, we go high,' I mutter to myself. But even the ballsy awesomeness of Michelle Obama can't touch the gloom that's hanging around my head like a cloud of midges. I swat around my ears as if I can dislodge it.

'Uh, Miss?'

'Hello, Veronica. I'm so glad you're here. I was a bit worried you'd boycott, being this close to the boys.'

She sighs with all the weariness of someone who has a second mortgage and thread veins, not a girl who should be obsessing over gel pens all day long. 'It kept me up last night, thinking about it. But I decided I am more loyal to my friends than I am annoyed by boys.' She borderline spits the last word out onto her ballet flats.

'Well… Everything is an experience. Think of it that way.'

'Is that how you think about the Hall falling to pieces?'

I scratch the back of my head and pull my jumper down a little further onto my hips. It's my best teal cashmere jumper: I might feel hopeless but I wouldn't let the Bluebells down by dressing that way tonight. 'Let's get inside, shall we?'

I thought I might be the first here. I was hoping I would be – to scope it out and pick out a good corner to lurk in while everyone else turned up. That way I could assess how I was going to get through this wholly awkward and shameful thing. And hopefully not batter Alex to death with his Scouts Annual 2017. The only plan I had so far was hiding between two crash mats, like a giant Connie toastie.

But nope. Here he is: Alex, surrounded by his minions in a big circle at his feet. The image of a dictator with very small ambitions.

'Ladies, please come right on in, make yourselves at home.' He beckons like an air traffic controller, as if we have a jumbo jet behind us.

'Thank you,' I manage.

There's a little bit of sizing up going on between Veronica and some of the boys, so I decide my only route is the high road – I can't let the girls down now by not modelling the mature way to do things.

'Scout Master.' I hold out my hand and dip into a curtesy.

'Erm, OK.' Alex shakes it.

OK, maybe I am squeezing a tiny bit of facetious-ness in there, with my maturity. But anything to make it through the next few hours.

The rest of my Bluebells start to file in slowly, with some anxious parents popping their faces round the door. When they see me they all produce the same sympathetic look, with a small frown and a head tilt. It starts to become funny in the way sad things shouldn't, but then do. I once laughed all the way through a rendition of 'All Things Bright and Beautiful' at a great-uncle's funeral.

And now I can feel the giggles bubbling at the base of my throat. So I do a head count as a distraction.

'All here.' I turn to Alex. 'Seeing as this is your domain, Scout Master, why don't we fit in with whatever you would normally be doing tonight? Bark studies, knot unpicking, tent dusting?'

I hear the titters of my sweet Bluebells as they realise I'm teasing.

But Alex seems unmoved. 'Actually, Mistress Bloom...' He puts one hand behind his back and bows in my direction. Pah. 'Here at the Hazlehurst Pack, we have a very special presentation to make to your troop. A unique performance, just for you. Isn't that right, Davey?'

A small dark-haired boy stands up just to my left and starts to speak with a squeaky wobble to his voice. 'This week we have been studying the history of female oppression throughout the ages, and the birth of femininim... Femiminimi... Of being fair to everyone. We would like to perform what we've learnt to you in a series of sketches.'

Little boys love serious drama like little boys love spinach for pudding.

'Do I have time to get a cushion, Scout Master?'

Alex smiles. 'But of course. And do take notes,' he says loudly and clearly, 'as you Bluebells will be the judges as to which boys deserve their arts badge from this task. Yes?'

'Yes!' the girls all sing back. Veronica even air punches, which may be her very first one.

And all of a sudden I am really looking forward to this evening.

–

It seems only fair to give Alex a hand with the tidying up as children are being collected from the front door. There was a lot of instrumental cross dressing as part of the sketches and now big white elasticated skirts have fallen over every surface, like discarded parachutes in the war on misogyny.

Those boys certainly went for it, so I will wipe the memory of their stupid chant at the fete from my mind. In fact, it feels so much easier at the moment to forget the entire fete.

After some furious blushing in the first five minutes, when the Scouts fully realised they couldn't fall back on fight scenes and gun mimes as they might in any other drama lesson, they got down to the matter at hand – a passionate Florence Nightingale at the battlefield hospital, a brave suffragette throwing herself under the king's horse, bras burned on the streets of London. Come to think of it, those first two did involve a few noisy death scenes and then in the third a boy called Francis got a bit carried away with the improvised nature of the scene and ran around screaming, 'Oh no, now my pants have caught fire! Help meeeee!' But by then the Bluebells were enjoying themselves so much they just cheered and applauded.

Each boy was awarded a badge in a quick ceremony at the end, just before the parents started turning up. And in all the activity, I didn't realise my batteries were once again recharging. No wonder the Matrix wants to harvest us – kids are really the most amazing source of energy.

I have my hands full of underskirts and cloth caps, and I'm holding the king's hobby horse under my chin to stop it toppling off.

'Let me take those from you, Connie.' It feels weird to hear Alex use my actual name. He stuffs all the assorted props into a big blue IKEA bag. 'That went well, I thought. Just enough public embarrassment to be both a punishment and a lesson.'

'Totally. Thank you. You didn't have to do that, but I know the girls appreciated it. So… yup, thanks.'

He swings the bag up and onto his shoulder, his bicep suddenly like a grapefruit under his sleeve. I can't seem to take my eyes off it. Maybe those *Bourne* DVDs of his come with a workout routine. 'The least I could do. Now, look, while we're here, I wanted to say, to clear some things up. You know, in all of this, I've never had a moment to explain my part in the—'

'Wait, that reminds me.' I scoop my book bag up from under one of the tables. 'I didn't think you'd mind me combining business and, er, well not pleasure as such… But anyway, I owe you this.'

I fish out the log book. My hands tremble as I push it towards him.

'Oh no, Connie. I don't need that. Not now.'

'Please take it.'

'No, honestly. I think from the uninhabitable state of the Hall, the Board can fairly rule that visitor numbers aren't making their quota.' He gives a sad shrug.

I push again in his direction. 'No, honestly, I insist. There's no use for it now. You might as file it with the rest of the Hall stuff.'

'I don't think—'

'I do!' I don't mean to push quite so hard, but the leather cover makes contact with his sweatshirt. 'Take it. The Hall is yours, anyway. I lost.'

Alex finally takes it in his hands, and presses his lips together into a dead straight line. He opens his mouth to speak but then something over my shoulder catches his eye. 'I think you've got a visitor. Do you mind locking up? All my Scouts are gone.' He takes the keys from his pocket and hands them over. It's like a very disappointing Secret Santa over here right now.

When I turn around, I see Flip in the doorway, her arms crossed and her foot tapping a fast, impatient rhythm. The grumpy look of her pose is somewhat spoiled by the huge fabric flowers she's customised her shoes with, and Gurpreet hopscotching around her.

Alex nods to Flip as he leaves, dragging his bag of props behind him. 'You two could form a double act, you know,' Flip starts. 'Glum and Glummer.'

'Gurpreet, love, could you do a very important job for me? I need you to check all the doors and windows are locked around the hut. Could you do that?'

She squeaks with excitement. 'Actual keys! My mum never lets me hold hers anymore!' Not a great sign, but I think Flip and I need some grownup time to get her very obvious grievances off her chest.

With Gurpreet heading for the broom cupboard, Flip hisses 'I can't believe you handed over the log book like that! Voluntarily! We should have been keeping that up our sleeve.'

I feel my battery draining all over again. Eighty per cent. Sixty... 'There's no more sleeve, Flip. No trouser leg, not so much as a glove. Nothing more to do. I tried to tell Dom, and Susannah. We had a great campaign and I'm so grateful for everything you did but—'

She lets out a snort. Her bright lipstick, usually always a beacon of cheer, on a pursed pout suddenly takes on a slightly scary look. 'But you're giving up. At this hurdle.'

'A hurdle of weight-bearing beams that are now on the floor of the Hall, yes. I just... Look, I don't know what you want me to say. I'll chain myself to the front doors? I'll gag Alex with a metre of bunting? I'll throw myself under the king's horse!?'

She puts her hands on her hips. 'I don't know what I want you to say, either. But I wanted you to fight, for the Hall, for all of us. You help bring this place together. You bring people together.'

'No, Flip, that was you. I just push a mop and make the tea, mostly.'

'Don't give me that nonsense! I used my PR tricks but you're the one that made me feel a part of the group, even as a newcomer. You're a bright spark, you're just also pretty good at hiding it. Behind your bloody mop. I… This whole thing really made me feel like part of the fabric round here. And now it's gone.' Her shoulders slump down a little. 'I miss it.'

I reach out and take her hand. 'So do I. Just because I know when to throw in the towel doesn't mean I didn't think it was an excellent towel. A towel I really really like. A lot.'

With a frown, Flip swings my hand a little. 'And just because I like you, doesn't mean I'm joining you in the towel throwing. I still think there's something there…'

'Ooh, what's towel throwing? Is it like welly wanging? Can we get a badge in it?' Gurpreet skips over, the keys tinkling as she goes.

'That's for next week. Everything locked tightly? Sure?'

The little lass nods solemnly.

'Good, because it's important everything is locked up tight. Leave the keys by the door for me. Thanks, love.'

Flip pulls on one of Gurpreet's long plaits. 'High time I got you home, lady. We're 15 minutes late for tea as it is and then your mum will be picking you up. And, Connie, please start using your phone again, hey?' She gives me a beady eye combined with a lopsided smile.

'Promise.' I put my hands to my heart. 'I swear on my best towel.'

I can tell there's so much more Flip would love to press me on, but the inescapable inevitability of teatime has saved my bacon. They hurry out together, little person rushing after big person.

I decide I owe it to Alex to really leave his place shipshape. Not just because of the awesome Feminism Half-hour, but because I might have been a bit brutal just before he left. He really didn't want to take that book, but I just couldn't bear to see it looking sadly out of place at home. Closure is what I'm after right now. Seeing as I don't have a job or a social campaign or – yes, Delilah, I do listen to you – any sort of romantic life, I think the first thing I need is closure. Even if it was handled with boxing gloves rather than kid ones.

I've washed up the squash beakers, I've sorted a few things in the broom cupboard so they no longer greet anyone opening the door with a dust pan in the face and I've put the lid back on about a million felt tips. I will expect a thank you card for that one. My last act of caretaking behind me after a half an hour blitz, I start to switch off the lights and make my way to the door.

But it doesn't open. I kick my feet around to find where Gurpreet has left the keys. But they're not there. Because she's locked it from the outside.

Oh balls. I'd obviously stressed locking everything a little too much and in her hurry to get back for jacket potatoes and beans Flip hasn't noticed what's happened. I scrabble in my bag for my phone. But calling Flip when she's probably running baths and digging out clean PJs would just be a pain. The same for Stevie. I don't want my mum panicking that I'm no longer capable of leaving a building on my own. And the rest of the Bunting Society are still pretty ratty with me. The only person I can think of who wouldn't mind sorting out this pickle is… Well, I have put the lids back on his felt tips. That counts for something.

After a very embarrassed/incredulous text exchange about my predicament, where I had to reassure Alex twice that I wasn't joking, he's on his way. So I sit with my back to the door, killing time by wondering how much worse my week could possibly get. I've just added 'dying for a toasted sandwich' and 'getting a bit chilly' onto my current list of misery. Next week's horoscope: just when you thought there was no more DOOM to be had…

'Connie?'

'I'm here. God, thanks so much. I'm starving—'

'Just before I let you out, I do want to say something.'

Dooooooom.

'OK! But you could say it when I'm on the other side of the door? The freedom side.'

His voice is a little muffled but absolutely confident. 'If I let you out before I say it, you'll cut me off again. Or assault me with a notebook or something. I absolutely have to say this.'

My forehead clonks onto the rough doorframe. 'Right. Great. I'll absolutely listen.'

'You said earlier that you lost. But this wasn't a war, not for me. I was doing my job, and I was trying to do it fairly.'

Doors are at least very useful for hiding rude hand gestures.

'You think I'm all about selling off properties for companies to make loads of money and that couldn't be more different from what I do. I'm working with the Estate because they don't have money. They give money to so many different charities and buildings, but it can't go on forever, that money. So someone like me comes in to manage it.'

'By snooping about behind our backs? By telling people the Hall was going to be a coffee shop any day now?'

There's a clonk from the other side of the wood. 'I had to find out how many people were actively using the Hall, whether it deserved those really crucial funds. You know the hospice in Castleview village? The Estate owns the building and they fund it. Well, they fund about 80 per cent of it. And so with a real cash flow problem, I was looking at each project with the exact same view – who was going to suffer if they lost their funding, if they had to move out of their building? Where can we get some essential funds from to keep the hospice operational? Unfortunately, Bluebell Hall didn't make it to the top of that list.'

'Where did we come?'

'Um, the bottom. Sorry. But there was an animal shelter and a program for supplying children's books to public buildings on there too. Good old Hibbs liked his charitable pursuits. I just wish he'd put as much effort into choosing financial advisors. His Estate is dangerously close to going broke. They're selling off the manor house, you know.'

I leap up and look through the spy hole. 'No way!'

I can just about make out Alex pushing a hand through his hair and kicking at the gravel. 'Way. I've just put it in the hands of the estate agent in the village, so expect the gossip to be all over Hazlehurst in at least seven minutes.' His mouth turns up into a rueful smile.

'There's probably already a text on my phone from Luce about it.'

'Yes, it's a relief to find today that your phone still works. That it hasn't met some awful sewing machine tragedy, or been melted by a hot glue gun. Because whenever I tried to reach you on Monday it didn't work.'

'Yes, thanks. I get it. I've had this lecture from everyone already. Message received. I won't do it again, Bluebell's honour.'

'Your friends were really worried about you. You're lucky to have them. And not just for the worrying bits. You guys always looked like you were having fun.'

He is making a really big hole in the gravel now. I remember what Stevie said over fish and chips – I should have been nicer to Alex, purely as someone who knew the ins and outs of the village and him being a brand new Billy no mates.

'Alex?'

'Yes?'

'Could I possibly come out now? I really am hungry.'

'Oh yes.' The heavy lock turns, and I'm free.

'Have you tried Flames N Chips yet? I know it sounds dodgy but the lamb kofta is actually amazing.'

It takes a moment for him to reply. 'Uh, um, yes. I mean, no, I haven't but I'd like to.'

'Right, then lock up and let's go!'

I can't change what's happened. I can't magically mend a roof with 50p and some Scotch tape. But I can keep the spirit of the Hall alive by making someone new to Hazlehurst feel like they have a friend.

Chapter 17

A kebab with Alex last night was actually not the stuff of nightmares, which really caught me off guard. His job as a financial consultant to charitable organisations has taken him to some pretty interesting places, but some heart-breaking ones too. As he put it, 'We only have charities because people seriously need them, and charities only run out of money because there are so many people still to help.' This might explain why his go-to demeanour is serious with a side of spread-sheet. And it's a pretty big lesson in why I shouldn't jump to conclusions about someone based on the fancy-pantsness of their clothes. I don't really think he does have that much money, going on the clapped-out nature of his Ford Fiesta. The shiny thing I saw him get into the other week might be a company car, I suppose.

He began to soften a bit over a jumbo lamb kofta and a can of Fanta, once we moved off heavy work topics and moved onto the rubbish children say, the terrible music they listen to and how we have essentially defined ourselves as old by not liking what they like.

'Although,' Alex pointed a chip for emphasis as he spoke, 'I caught Greg Moon humming a song from *Frozen* the other day. And I have to admit the soundtrack is pretty catchy.'

I had silently munched my way through a suspiciously stale slice of cucumber at that point, having only just recently learned my lesson about assuming, judging and generally not being Cool with Stuff.

'I have three nieces!' he spluttered in reply, when he saw my 'no judgement' face. 'I can't believe you see a group of girls every week and you don't know all the words to 'In Summer'. Just download it. Trust me. You'll love it.'

So now I am sneakily listening to YouTube in the library, with my headphones plugged into the dusty old PC in the corner. As the strategically missed punchlines in the song hit me, I swallow my giggles and open a new tab. Time to take back control. Time to find a plan. Somewhere. Google search: *what to do when you don't know what to do with your life.*

No, that's just too sad sounding. Delete delete delete.

Find a new career before you're 30.

I mean, technically, I have a few months yet. Just.

Axed caretaker seeks exciting new role. Must be local, flexible hours and ridiculously good pay.

Well, Noel Edmonds believes in Cosmic Ordering. And he has the carefully groomed facial hair of a very rich man.

I switch back to Olaf and his snowy twinkle toes, and hit replay. They should have this on loop at the job centre. It takes the edge off the gut churning search for a job when you know you're up against a thousand other applicants and your CV was last updated when McBusted was a thing.

Searching at the library seemed a sensible choice – a few of Mum's friends had come over with freshly baked biscuits and lots of sympathy. They know when she hits a rocky patch that she needs time and chat and support, even if it doesn't seem to make a difference on the surface. It does, though, it really does. I can tell her sleep pattern is off from the rumbling boil of the kettle coming up through the floorboards at 2 a.m., and she's pulled out of a few shifts at work. She keeps telling me not to worry, that she's coming through it. But I have my eye on her, all the same.

Her mates were setting up shop in the living room with mugs of tea and a box of tissues at the ready, so I thought it best to leave them to it and do some job research down the road. But now the enforced silence of the library is feeling like so much more of a distraction than Sheila's loud stories about her Awful Aunt Doreen or the new recycling bin day. It's this big empty thing hanging around me, taking up all the air in the place. It's like a rogue bouncy castle has been kicked inside the double doors and someone is sneakily and quietly inflating it around me, blocking my escape, weighing me down onto the wonky swivel chair and bouncing back at me the lame quality of my brainstorming session so far.

I could work with children? A CRB check and the ability to make hats out of newspaper does not an educator make. Besides, how would you pay to retrain and still chip in for the bills?

Maybe a museum, then, as a curator. Or tour guide. Pretty sure people have actual degrees in curating to do that. And have you seen a major museum around here lately? No, you'd have to go to a city, and leave Mum behind. You'd have to start all over again. New job, new place, new people.

I could try music journalism again. Yes, and when they ask you to describe the last gig you went to, you can say how the accordion music was tinny but at least the ribbon plaited up nicely all down the pole. Cool.

Flip said maybe I could take some of the skills from the Bunting Campaign, turn that into a job. Oh yeah. Cos that will look smashing on a CV. 'I ran a campaign to save a building that fell apart anyway.

But we did make some nice bunting. Ignore the other candidates with experience and education. Pick me!'

I turn the monitor's volume up a few bars. Olaf can even trump an inner voice with a mean streak.

After checking Facebook every third second and taking a personality test to reveal which of the Golden Girls I was most like (Bea), and checking Facebook once more to absorb pictures of Claire's new baby again, I had a last-minute brainwave to check the local Hazlehurst forum. Not just a place for people to vent about hedge heights or Bonfire Night starting too late in the evening (the clue's in the name, guys), it also has some For Sale stuff and a few job ads.

Something instantly catches my eye:

> Love working with children? Local person sought for flexible job.

I click through with my tongue pinched between my teeth.

> Nanny needed for professional couple and their adorable son. No official qualifications required but passion and dedication a must. I'm a stay-at-home mum but due to my fashion business taking off, I need some childcare help. Also some light cooking and cleaning

duties. Please call Annabel for more
information and to supply references.
You'll love Alfred when you meet him!

Alfred. The name stirs an uncomfortable memory. I
click the attachment and there he is – the screamer
from a Funday way back when, the one who most
certainly did not care for my vocal talents and
dismissed me with a tone Simon Cowell would have
found a bit harsh. In the background of the picture-
perfect image was one of the uber-yummy mummies,
frolicking with her equally yummy husband at what
looked like a National Trust property.

Could I be a nanny? I can't pretend it's ever really
been a dream of mine. But they're local. And they
look like they could pay a fair wage. And I could still
be around for Mum. It's not a boring office job. I
wouldn't end up humiliated and heartbroken. That's
something.

But I'd be one-on-one with a baby who isn't
exactly a bouncing bundle of joy, and pushing a
Hoover around and cooking someone else risotto for
their tea. A big gang of Bluebells is fun because there's
action and noise and laughter and Bieber discussions.
I'm not sure Alfred is down with *Now 53!* just yet. Do
I have it in me to be a full time Mary Poppins? She
was magical, for Chrissakes, and even she moved on
after a few weeks of work.

I could flip-flop on this forever, surrounded by the Dewey decimal system and the big dusty rubber tree in the corner. I've been soul searching on and off for months about what I should do with my life and I'm no closer to some magical epiphany. So I snatch up my phone. I need an opinion. But not Stevie's, I know what he'll say without saying it. And I can't ask Susannah, just another disappointment to her and Gran. Or Flip.

So sod it. I can weigh it up later, when I'm presenting my references. I quickly dash out a text to the number before I can let any more wibbles into my head.

With most of 'In Summer' committed to memory, I figure I should let someone else use the prehistoric PC for their important work (printing out Sudukos and directions to the nearest Harvester by the look of the printer). So I head home, ready to supply Mum with her fifteenth cup of tea and absorb the damage of her morning's heart-to-hearts.

But instead of Mum folding herself into the corner of the sofa in her dressing gown, I find her upstairs, packing an overnight bag. There's a warm glow to her cheeks as she lays some pants and vests into her little red hold-all. 'Hello love!'

'Hello. Um, are you off somewhere?'

Mum moves behind me to get to her wardrobe doors. 'Yes, it's all a bit last minute. But Sheila's brother has this place in Devon. Lovely house, ten minutes from the sea. So, he's broken his leg.'

'Hang on, what?'

She puts a Jojo Moyes paperback down on top of her neatly pressed jeans. 'He needs a hand getting about for a while and Sheila said, why don't I come with her? Get some sea air. I'm not down for any shifts till Tuesday. And once she said it, I thought Yes. That's what I need. Some new scenery. So you've got the house to yourself, isn't that nice?' She nudges me in the ribs gently. 'You could have people round. You never do that. Or you could have a weekend away. See some friends. We both need some distractions, hey?' For just a minute she lays her head on my shoulder and squeezes me round the middle. 'Sometimes I worry that you do too much, Connie, love. For me, I mean, since Gran's been gone.'

I open my mouth, ready to match my frown with an objection in words, but she quickly keeps going.

'Don't get me wrong, when you came home then you were the one face I wanted to see. You are, you have always been my sunshine.' She smoothes my bob down on one side and tries to curl the ends up with her fingers. 'But what makes you happy? Who makes you happy? Someone just for you, to be your sunshine. That's what I want for you, darling. You shouldn't worry about the clouds in my sky, love. They clear away, they always do.'

I study the greying laces on my Converse and shuffle my feet about on Mum's purple throw rug.

She sighs. 'I don't know if I said as much back then, but that Manchester bloke was just a total pillock, scuse my French. And not only did he dare to break your heart but he told you you weren't good enough for the job. Pfft.' She lets out a snort that causes her chestnut-brown fringe to fluff up in the air. 'You can do anything. I've always known that. Everything you achieved with Bluebell Hall shows that.'

I feel this might not be the time to tell Mum I'm considering being an au pair at twenty-nine.

Mum smiles broadly and then she's off again, putting Elizabeth Arden perfume and breath mints into her bag. 'I hope we get some nice spring sun!'

'Yes,' I flop down onto her bed, 'me too.'

—

A completely quiet house is an eerie thing. I mean, I can be home on my own really happily but it's usually just before Mum's coming in or I'm about to go out. It's a temporary thing. But this new quiet is starting to feel like the library again. Permanent. Like a new rule I'm going to have to live by. I put the telly on to fill the air. A *Grand Designs* repeat. Some things fall apart and some things go wrong, but you can always count on Kevin McCloud in a nice jumper, looking at some weathered copper sheeting in 2003. But when he starts pulling sceptical faces at the roof, I get a heavy feeling in my stomach and flashbacks of wet shoes and flapping pigeons, so I switch it off again.

Who can I get round? Or who could I go and visit? The thought of yet another conversation about why I shouldn't give up on Bluebell Hall puts me off getting the Bunting guys round. And I don't want to eat into Stevie and Luce's quality time more than I do; they're always working so hard and doing so much with Abel.

Maybe I should get away. Maybe being far from the Hall would be pretty healthy for a few days. And Mum's clearly sorted – she'll be dusting crutches and digging in the sand before the day's out. I have been meaning to catch up with my old Manchester flatmates – Claire especially, I didn't even see her while she was pregnant and now little Freddie is two months old.

I tap out a WhatsApp message to her:

> Fancy a very tidy houseguest for the
> weekend? I can bring wine and Doritos.
> Also can do nappies if gloves are
> provided.

I didn't expect a reply right away but one pops up:

> Yes! Ork.

Must be a typo for OK but I'll take it. I tell her that I'll
be there tonight and go off in search of the spare keys
for Mum's car and my toothbrush. Catching up with a
great mate is exactly the kind of soothing balm my life
needs right now, like itch relief cream when you've
been attacked by mozzies on holiday. Claire is a great
listener, a great advice giver, and more importantly
she doesn't hog the Doritos.

Chapter 18

When I reach Claire's terraced house, I squeeze into a parking space on my eighth attempt and clamber to her front door, wine bottles clinking in a carrier bag hanging from my wrist. But it's not the soothing, listening, calm friend of my Manchester days who opens the door. It's her horror movie evil twin, who's clearly been locked in the attic with no access to a shower, clean clothes or a comfy bed.

The hair on one side of her head is matted and stiff, while grease makes the other side droopy and lank. I may have been her mate through the terrible hair gems trend of the 00s but this is something else. I try to bite back the shock at her egg-stained joggers (Claire works as a fashion buyer, so I usually count on her for a style injection). I can't really make out what she's wearing on her top half as there's a funny tangle of fabric going around her middle and her back, then over her shoulders. She's also bouncing on the spot, which is pretty distracting.

'Connieeeeeee!' she whispers excitedly. 'I would hug and scream but the Ork has only just fallen asleep. And if I stop bouncing he'll wake up and kill me.' She nods like this is a totally normal thing to say about a newborn. All I can see of him is two little chocolate-coloured feet swaying in time to the bounces, at her waist. 'But thank god you're here!'

I think she is lunging forward to greet me, but instead she yanks the bag so forcefully off my wrist that she scrapes some of my skin with it.

'God, I can't remember when I last ate. Come in, come in!'

She bounces on her toes as she leads me down the hallway, giving me an only just audible tour of the place. 'Living room. Downstairs loo. And here's the kitchen. This is where I live now.'

If I had been in any doubt that this couldn't be the Claire I'd known, the kitchen definitely brought back uni nostalgia by the bucket-load. Big bucket-load of washing up, that is. The two of us could never keep so much as a side plate clean, and in the end our parents had cracked and shared the cost of a weekly cleaner. This was back in the days before either of us had any shame.

She holds up one hand, like a policeman stopping traffic. 'Now, don't you dare offer to clean this up for me. Just don't. I know it's a state, but the Ork really doesn't leave me much time between jiggling and feeding and poo explosions and weight checks. Occasionally I get to brush my teeth,' she half-laughs, half-whispers but I think we both know it's pretty close to reality. 'Just, please, don't offer.'

I hadn't planned on any such thing but by the way she's repeating it, I think I know what I need to do.

Pulling on a pair of marigolds I spot poking out of the Kitchen Aid bowl, I shake my head. 'You just do your bouncing there, hun, I'll get some suds going and you can tell me all about it.'

Over a very stubborn lasagne crust that I think might be older than Freddie, Claire lovingly explains his nickname. 'You know Anton is just a massive *Lord of the Rings* nut? We had those Elf ears for everyone at the wedding, remember? Well, when he saw Freddie come out – and I mean actually come out – he said with all the white goo and screaming, he looked like an Ork being pulled out of the mud by Saruman. And since then, he's not really disappointed on the human-hating, destructive side.'

'Awww.' I scrub at some welded-on bechamel.

Claire's hands flap above her messy head. 'I mean I LOVE him, I do. I LOVE the fuzzy hair on his shoulders and the way he burps. I cannot get enough of the smell of his neck. But you start to have mixed feelings about anyone who screams at you in the dark every two hours. And with Anton having to go to the States for work at the last minute, it was like fate that you messaged me. Thank you. I know I look a state.'

'You do not.'

'I do. But I appreciate that you would lie to my face like this. That's true friendship. But, man, where has the time gone? It seems like yesterday we were all in Wainwright Road, playing guess the mystery meat from the Shangri-La Kebab House. Staying up till the wee hours to smash our Mario Kart records. And now I would kill for a digestive and an eight p.m. bedtime. I'm so sorry I haven't been in touch. What with the preggy puking and getting ready to go on leave… and now being dominated by a person smaller than a house cat. I've been a rubbish friend.'

I turn and poke her with a soapy yellow finger. 'You haven't. I have. I should have come to see you ages ago. The minute you weed on that stick. I just got caught up with stuff at home.'

Claire took the risky move of perching on a tall stool and just jogging herself with one foot against the floor. Freddie's head whips from one side to the other and he gurgles in his sleep, but doesn't actually wake. She looks like she's just cut the right wire on a huge ticking bomb. I let out my held breath.

'Yes, so tell me about that. I saw you tagged in something about your Hall closing. That can't be happening, can it?'

My shoulders shrug as I focus on oil-like coffee dregs in about eight different mugs. 'It isn't right, but it's happening. It's happened, in fact. I had to give up the keys. The roof caved in. Pretty final, all in all. But I'm not here to talk about that, I'm here to talk about you. Maybe we could look up Tallie and Hungry Dave. Are they still about? I could cook us all lunch tomorrow, if you don't mind. I'd love to know what everyone's getting up to. And we could play pass the Ork, give you a break. What do you think?'

I turn round to gauge whether this would all be a bit much for Claire, and she's asleep, mouth dropped open, head leaning back against the tiled kitchen wall. I take her hand and gently pull her up and towards the living room.

With Claire safely zonked out in her rocking chair, Freddie still papoosed on her front, I set about doing exactly what I had intended to get away from: being her caretaker. I finished the washing up, then I blitzed the kitchen surfaces and floor. I changed her bed, put a load of washing on, sorted out a blockade of clean baby clothes that had amassed just by the nursery door. I didn't risk putting the radio on and as I found one little job after another to absorb me, the silence trailed behind my steps, stirring up the crappy little inner voice again.

So, you might make a decent nanny, then. That's something.

And as I collect up all the water glasses and mugs and half-eaten bits of Nutella on toast from the living room, all the while terrified one clinking tumbler might ruin this temporary peace, I don't know how to argue with that voice. I am good at taking care of things, of people, maybe I should get wise and at least charge properly for it.

There's an empty tub of Ben & Jerry's on the mantelpiece, with a sticky pool of its remains running all the way down the wall below. With some Dettol wipes it's history, and I start dusting down all Claire's photos and nick nacks while I'm there. Here she is with her sister, both gap-toothed, childish grins turned towards a busy pier. Oh my god, here I am, with my awful centre parting and bum-length hair that I had as a Fresher still. I remember Claire's mum taking this picture, on the day we both moved into halls. I think it was a way to just get her to stand close to the other stragglers who'd found the bar, and make us introduce ourselves with stammers and sweaty cheeks. It worked. Her wedding picture also stirs up great memories of a pick-and-mix sweet buffet, cracking house music in the early hours and bacon butties at dawn. But clearly, from Anton's kilowatt smile as he gazes down at his beautiful bride, I didn't enjoy it half as much as they did.

There's one of those frames with different squares for different photos and each one has a blissful holiday snap. I can make out New York, maybe Thailand, and Prague, I think. All the different city skylines and beaches and sunsets are united by Claire and Anton holding hands in each one.

Right at the end of the mantelpiece, a small trophy holds up a black and white image. It's a tiny Triathlon prize from 2015. I never knew these guys were so sporty. And the image behind is one of those fuzzy baby scans – Freddie's first appearance in his family's photo gallery.

I thought I would come away to Manchester and catch up with my old life, get away from the Hall and everything at home. But even if I was a triathlete I wouldn't be able to catch up with missing so much. Even if I could run like a cheetah. While I've been jogging on the spot back in Hazlehurst, Claire and the others have been sprinting ahead, doing so much, so many different things. Our old glory days on Wainwright Road are just a small chunk of their exciting lives, and it's long gone.

What would my photo gallery look like? There'd be me and Mum, me and Stevie, then me holding

Abel as a little red-faced bundle in a crocheted blanket. There'd be me with Gran's old ramshackle tool kit, trying to fix a light switch with my tongue held between my teeth. And one of Flip, Susannah, Lucy and me at the fete, too busy talking up our cause to smile for a photo. But what's next? Where will I be smiling from in a year's time?

I hardly feel like smiling now, so I can't really see how that would go.

And as if he can totally read my mind, Freddie lets out a loud squawk from Claire's chest, and she bolts instantly upright. 'Wha... What?!'

'It's fine, it's just your sweet Ork. You've been asleep for nearly two hours, you know. I should have taken a pic for your mantelpiece. Now, what can I get you?'

Claire sinks back into her chair cushions, now her mum radar can switch off with no fires or wild cats or dropped babies in the vicinity. 'I'm going to have to feed him, so a big glass of water would be amazing. And if there are any of those digestives left... Oh you tidied! You angel! You're like my own Mary Poppins!'

Well, if I was looking for a sign of what to do next, maybe I've found it.

–

We both turned in early, soon after a takeaway pizza and a few beers (me) and a whole pint of orange juice (Claire). Freddie stuck to his special reserve.

After the third set of apologies that Freddie was up screaming again, at 3.15 a.m. I told Claire it really really was no bother and to let me walk the house with him. He likes stairs, it seems, especially going up them. My thighs don't like it, but he does and my thighs' screams are much easier to ignore. It felt good to see Claire's eyes wrinkle up in relieved happiness that she could flop down on her pillows and grab some essential sleep. Plus, I couldn't get a wink anyway. My mind was on full whir, trying to remember any good risotto recipes and working out how to slip Alfred chocolate buttons until he warmed to me. I'd had a response from his yummy mummy, asking for more details and asking plainly at the end of the message: *Are you the same Connie Duncan from Bluebell Hall, as was?* So how exactly I answered that without coming across desperate or a real loser or downright pissed off was going to be its own challenge. But it was a job, a way forward at least. And anything had to be better for me than more standing still. So I gritted my teeth and I wrote an email devoid of emotion, listing all my experience and my skills. And selling myself as something I wasn't really sure I wanted to be.

Claire had been really buoyed when I repeated my idea of trying to get some of the old crew together for an ad hoc lunch at hers. She put down the ground rules that all the food had to be on her and instantly munchable, so we didn't make any unnecessary washing up. That sounded good to me, so I set out for a Sainsbury's to collect five different kinds of hummus and all the pittas they had. And as I'm pushing the trolley, I have a missed call from Flip.

Maybe the mum's gossip network had sprung into life this morning and she already knew about my nanny application? Judging by the fact that everyone knew Stephanie Pritchard's mum had broken her arm at judo (in a fight over the last pack of Wheat Crunchies in the vending machine) before the plaster had even set on her cast, this was completely possible.

While I'm loading the bags into the car, I get a text from Susannah.

> Please call me. Thank you.

Weird, I didn't know that she could text. But I don't have the energy for talking to her about what a disappointment I am again. Freddie's cries are still ricocheting about my brain and I want to get back and lose myself in nostalgia with old mates. Even if I have to bounce about a mini Ork as I do it. Blimey, that kid can cry.

I can feel my phone vibrating as I park painfully slowly at Claire's again. Someone is ringing and ringing and ringing and it's putting me off my crunchy manoeuvre. I'm just grunting at the screen, about to turn it off now the handbrake is safely on, when I see it's Dom. I still feel guilty about how we spoke the other day in the chip shop, so it would be really rubbish to ignore him now.

Before I can even get out my 'Hey Dom,' he cuts across me.

'Have you seen Polly?! She's missing.'

Chapter 19

I set the orange bags down on the kitchen table with my phone pressed into my ear as I fire questions at Dom. 'When did you last see her? Or hear from her? And she won't answer her phone? And nothing from her friends?'

Dom answers with an even but reedy voice: he's clearly been asked this stuff so much today that's it's like he's reading a script. 'I don't even know who her friends are these days, she never tells me. She's disappeared before but never overnight. I don't even know how much money she's got on her. She left for school as normal yesterday but they say she never got there. I had to call... I had to call the police, you know.'

He suddenly stops talking and it sounds like he's put the phone down.

'Dom? Dom, look, I'm not in the village but I can get back, in three or four hours. Just wait for me and we'll...'

He's back again. 'No, you stay put. I just hoped maybe she'd said something to you. She always seemed brighter after you two talk. You have that way with the girls. But if she does ring—'

'I will be straight onto you, in a heartbeat. Are you sure you don't want me around? We could go out, look around the parks, knock on a few doors?'

He sighs. 'We've done it. Flip, and her fella, and Susannah. Steve and Alex, even. We've done this village and the ones she could have got to easily on the school bus. But if she got a train into London...'

I didn't leave him any time to linger on such a huge and scary possibility. 'She won't have. I bet it's a sleepover with a new mate and in the excitement about watching blogger beauty tips all night she just forgot to tell you. She'll be back under your roof with over-plucked eyebrows in no time.'

I really don't feel as jolly about this as I'm trying to sound.

'I have a tracking device all ready for her ankle when she does show up.' Dom's hollow chuckle comes quietly down the line.

I can hear wailing from Claire's bedroom. The hummus is getting sweaty in the bags.

'Let me know, just as soon as you know. And remember what I said about coming back. I'd be really happy to.'

'Yup. OK. Thanks, then.'

Dom rings off and I can imagine him instantly springing up, keys in hand, to make another tour of the village, eyes peeled for a burgundy ponytail swishing around the next corner.

Just teenage hijinks, I think sternly. She's got some new cool mate and she's too wrapped up in it to be anything other than stupid and selfish and short-sighted. Classic teen nonsense. When I was fifteen I queued all night for Foo Fighters tickets without telling Mum first (mostly because I knew she'd say no) and imagine poor Mum's experience. I didn't have a mobile then either, and no sneaky Facebook app to track a teen. A shiver of remembered guilt works its way down my back. I hope Mum's having a blast on the beach, I think, because she deserves a lifetime of holidays for her maternal services.

Hijinks, hijinks, hijinks, I keep thinking, to block out the scariest thoughts. I repeat it like a mantra you'd get from a yoga teacher in a *Carry On* movie. It fills my head as I push Freddie in his pram round the local park, so Claire can have a slow bath. I think it so I don't think about car accidents or muggings or head traumas. It pops up in between the sound of crisps crunching as our old mates assemble and we dive into dips and reminiscence. I think it every time I check my phone for news from Dom, or from any of the others back at home. Hi-bloody-jinks. The pittas are munched, the drinks drunk, the baby cooed over and cuddled with. And I'm thinking: just some hijinks. Absolutely.

And although I drink in my Manchester friends like the sorely needed tonic they are, I feel like this is already a memory I'm replaying from a distance. Because it doesn't feel like my real life. My real life is back in Hazlehurst. It's with my Hazlehurst friends who are sick with worry, while I'm watching Hungry Dave mime that time he ate an entire wheel of cheese. This will be a memory I turn to when I'm sad or bored or a bit lonely, like you think of an amazing birthday cake. But you don't need it every day. You need the bread and butter of your real life, the rough with the smooth, not just frosting and chocolate sponge.

I feel so warm and satisfied now I've taken in a big slice of these guys – all doing do well with jobs or families or obsessive hobbies they're mad keen on, and Claire has a light in her eyes when she holds Freddie that I've never seen in her before – but this isn't my life any more. It's a big part of what's made me me, but I can't get it back. We'll never eat Domino's every day for a week again, because we know that way heart attacks lie. We won't be obsessing over why someone's new crush hasn't called them, because half of us are married. There's no midnight ping-pong because there are eight a.m. meetings.

Whatever answers I'm looking for about my future, I can't find by cosying up in nostalgia about my past. I might be heartbroken when I'm in Hazlehurst but it's my here and now. And right now my friends there need me. I ran away from Manchester all those years ago because things went horribly wrong and my dreams were crushed. And now I realise that all I ran away from back then was the good friends who had been there, supporting me. And I'm not about to make that mistake again: so my plans for the Hall crumbled? Doesn't mean my amazing friendships in Hazlehurst will. Not if I have anything to say about it.

'I'm really sorry, Claire, guys,' I say, wiping pitta crumbs on my jeans. 'I think I have to get back. A mate at home has got some stuff going on.'

Claire gives me a lopsided smile. I can tell she'd love me to stick around for more catching up (and cleaning up) but I've also caught her watching me check my phone for the 700th time today, so she must know something's up.

'Fair enough. Mary Poppins always knows when her work is done. I hope that umbrella of yours gets you home quick. Thanks for everything, Con.'

–

At a service station outside Milton Keynes, I'm checking my tires and filling the tank. I want to blast the rest of the way home, with no interruptions. I'm just dumping my Red Bull, Wotsits and M&Ms on the passenger seat as my essential road fuel, when my phone buzzes against the dashboard.

Dom's voice rattles off a breathless sentence.

'Hey, hey. Slow down. Start again. She's where?'

'Coventry. With my mother-in-law. Her gran. I'm leaving now. Just wanted to tell you, in case you were worried.'

'I was but… Coventry, I'm really close to Coventry. I can get there faster, and bring her straight to you. Shall I do that? I'd really like to.'

'Yes, thank you, Connie. Yes, please.'

–

'Do I need to put the child lock on or are we cool? You're not going to ditch me at the lights, are you?'

Polly rolls her eyes but it doesn't detract from how red and puffy they are. They match those of her poor old gran, Margaret, who gave me five cups of tea when I arrived at the address Dom supplied.

'She told me her dad put her on the train. She told me she had a half term coming up and of course I always love to see her. It's hard for me to get down to where they live now, my hip isn't what it used to be. But I never thought... I mean, poor Dominic. The worry! I know... What that worry is like as a parent... You see...' She sobbed into a Jaffa cake and Polly hung her head that little bit lower.

'It'll all come out in the wash!' I chirruped with false confidence as I rubbed the gran's arm and made soothing shushing noises. I was just grateful she didn't need carrying up and down the stairs like Freddie to distract her from crying – my thighs were well and truly burned out.

After more apologies from Margaret – who'd only twigged that Polly was on the run when she happened to check her ginormous old answer machine – and corned beef sandwiches for our tea, I loaded one duffel bag and one anxious teen into Mum's car. I didn't want to leave the old dear in a state but I knew Dom would be climbing the walls till Polly was safely at home and under her purple bedspread once more.

When we hit the motorway, I couldn't take the silence anymore.

'So why don't you tell me the story of your life?'

'Eh?'

'It's a line from *When Harry Met Sally*. It was made way before your time, slightly before mine, actually, but it's a classic. I can lend it to you, if you like. These two people have a long car ride ahead of them so to pass the time, they tell each other a potted life story. So why don't you tell me how you ended up with your gran under false pretences? You're going to have to explain it to your dad, and possibly a police officer,' Polly shrinks down further in her seat, 'so you might as well practise on me.'

Her eyes remain trained on the window as the motorway lights whiz by in the dark.

'Fine. I can go first. I was in Manchester today, before I came to get you.'

Polly frowns and turns towards me. She picks at her lime green nails.

'It's where I went to uni, and I worked there for a few years after. Till I made a fool of myself and got my heart stomped on. Some of my best friends live there still. And I think,' I keep my eyes trained on the lights of the car in front as I think of the right words, 'I think I was running away by going there. I didn't like what was going on back in the village so I ran away. To something more fun, somewhere I felt safe. Where I felt like me again.'

'Watch *Oprah* much?' Polly's deadpan delivery is A+ teenager material. 'I wasn't running away, God.' She draws this last word out into at least four syllables, in a way that can only be done by someone aged twelve to seventeen. 'I wanted to see Gran because it's the only place I can talk about Mum without feeling bad. I know Dad would rather just sweep it all under the carpet and never say her name again. But Gran tells me stories about mum, from when she was my age. She shows me old pictures, she even has some of Mum's crazy eighties clothes. When I talk to Gran, it's the next best thing. To her.'

Now I'm staring at the Toyota in front because I'm trying to keep the tears in my eyes. This was no idle burst of hijinks. This was a lonely girl trying to get back to her mum.

'So, when you were disappearing out, and your dad thought it was with new mates, you were...'

'With my gran. Yeah, I know it's lame. But. Whatevs.'

I swallowed hard. 'I bet your dad would go with you to do that, any day of the week. You nearly gave him a heart attack, you know.'

Polly's cheek bunches up where she's biting it on the inside. She just nods in reply.

'He loves you.'

'I know,' she manages in a small croak. 'But he doesn't get it. When he sees Gran they both get really sad and they don't want to get into all that so they talk about pointless stuff like the weather and traffic. But when it's just me and her, we can talk about the good things. And even the crying is good then. Does that sound weird?'

'Nope. Not at all. There is definitely such a thing as good crying.' Wow. This girl is operating on a level of emotional maturity I'm not sure I could find on a good day.

'I didn't want to hurt him. And I shouldn't take it out on him at home, but sometimes I need to dig it all up, think about Mum and remember her. It won't bring her back, I know, but it's better than nothing. It's better than pretending she was never here. That's what he does.'

A white BMW rushes past us in the fast lane. 'I don't think that's what he's doing, love. I think that's just his only way of coping. Or maybe he feels just like you do – that he'd like to talk about her but he doesn't want you to get sad? But really there's only one way to find out…'

'Talk to him,' Polly says in a wobbly voice. 'I figured that's where you were going with this.'

'Pass me some M&Ms then.' I throw back the handful she gives me. 'OK, so you and your dad are going to talk about you guys and your life, when you get home. But right now you've got to keep me awake till we get there. If you don't want to tell me your life story, why not tell me your mum's. Tell me everything you learned from your Gran. Start at the beginning, don't leave anything out.'

—

I think I would have really liked Polly's mum, if I'd had the chance to meet her. Apparently she used to go to all the festivals she could as a teenager, and she was really into Madonna and Prince when she was Polly's age. Had the lace gloves and everything. She used to rescue battered songbirds from the neighbour's cat and feed them bacon rind till they were better. She met Dom at a drunken house party, when they both reached for the last can of cider, and they fell in love at first sight.

Polly spoke clearly and happily about her mum all the way home, the stories getting richer and warmer the further south we went. As we drove into Hazlehurst she wound down an anecdote about her mum breaking her ankle in a pair of white stilettos.

'Grandpa never let her live it down, Gran said.'

'I bet. And quite rightly.'

'So… Are you going to tell me the full story of your life?'

I blow a big breath of air up through my fringe. 'Well then I'd just send us both to sleep, and that wasn't the point.'

'It's funny, though.' Polly traces a finger round and round on the window. 'I had to get to Coventry – on my own – to find the thing I'd lost. I had to go there to keep my mum alive, in my mind, I mean. But the thing you've lost is right on your doorstep and you're just… whatever.'

'Polly, it's not that simple…'

She gives me a blank stare. 'I'm not saying you can save the Hall single-handedly. You can't, like, magic-ally win the lottery and buy it back. But you don't have to cut it out so harshly. You can remember it. Keep it with you. You could say a proper goodbye.'

We pull up outside their house and the front curtains twitch. A second later, Dom is at the door, waving madly.

'It's wrapped up in you, like we wrapped the high street in bunting that time. You can't just ignore that.'

I'm completely spellbound by what she's said and sit there like a right lemon, immobile, long after she's finished hugging Dom fiercely on the doorstep. The only thing that jolts me out of my coma is a text. From Annabel:

> We've just had a busy weekend at a fashion trade show and desperately need help sooner rather than later. We're seriously considering you for the post. Can you come tomorrow for an interview and face-to-face with Alfred?

Chapter 20

With Mum still living it up on the coast with ice cream cones and broken legs, there was no one to disturb with my five a.m. run first thing on Monday morning. Polly had spent all of Sunday talking with Dom, really talking by the sounds of her texts (after I had Googled some of the weirder abbreviations. *IU2U* felt a bit like it was harder work than just typing *It's Up To You*, but hey, I'm clearly old). I'd spent Sunday sending a lot of texts and emails to get my new life order up and running. Firstly another one to Annabel, sorting out an interview filling her in about me. And then a whole lot more. It's time to make a change, and one that I choose for myself, rather than one that just happens to me.

I spent a lot of time staring at the giant pile of bunting that had been rescued from the sludgy hall store room. It had a slight whiff of damp but that wasn't what made my stomach turn in knots. Was I really going to do this?

I was. I really was.

The last thing I had to do before my run, before everything kicked off, was to send a message to Alex. He wasn't going to like this, but it had to be done. What Polly said had really hit home. I had run away from the Hall for the last time. Now I was facing the truth – and head on.

With my message swooshing its way to him, my trainers on my feet and a heavy rucksack on my back, it was time to hit the streets.

–

'What on EARTH are you doing?! I thought I explained all this!'

Alex is trying to keep his voice low and steady, but it's not working. Stress is making him squeaky. I know a little something about stress, as Flip tied my arms just that bit too high up, and now they're really starting to ache. But then, who said being a human barricade was easy? It can be pretty, if you're as wrapped up in bunting as I am, but it won't be easy.

'Bluebell Hall, for one, for all!' Susannah shouts right in Alex's ear as she stomps past, her handmade sign held proudly at head height. He winces and then takes a full step back as Flip and her kids run in front of him, their hands linked in a human crocodile. Her two littlest ones have decorated T-shirts that say 'Bluebell Hall a coffee shop? You're having a latte!'

Alex ruffles his already bed-ruffled hair. It's 7.30 a.m. and he clearly leapt straight out of bed when he saw my early morning text and shot over here. I think his crumpled Iron Man top might be the one he sleeps in. It's weirdly cute.

But his face is about as cute as a charging bull's. 'You know what's going on here, Connie. I'm not sitting on a fat pile of cash. I'm just trying to keep the charity above water.'

I beckon him closer in my direction, with a twitch of my head. My hands are, after all, bound by bunting to the front gate. 'I know that,' I say very softly, catching a smell of something lemony from his neck. 'I know the Hall is sold. But I don't want to go quietly, sorry. Consider this my very loud goodbye. And I figured, if we could get a little publicity for the Hibbert Foundation, and how it's doing so much good stuff with so little money, that couldn't hurt?'

Alex blinks and loosens his scowl. 'Oh.'

'Thing is, we've got some more of Flip's mates joining us with their kids on the school run, any time soon. And the OAP choir, once they've had their tea and toast and get minibussed down. Our sixth-formers, if they can convince the bus driver to make an extra stop. So that will make a decent crowd for the journalist and his photographer to capture. A decent human interest piece, *Bunting Society Goes Barmy for Great British Charity*. Something like that.'

Alex blinks some more. And then he smiles, just a little. 'Well, what can I do?'

'Play the part of disgruntled suit, if you don't mind, for that bit more drama, and,' I twitch my head again so he leans in towards me and that citrus smell tickles my nose, 'I actually have this really annoying itch on my inner wrist, if you could?'

'An opportunist to the last.' Alex rolls his eyes, but in a soft, indulgent way. 'Fine. I'm going to go home, get changed into actual clothes and then come back with a fake strop on. But please tell Susannah to stop shouting at me; it's pretty alarming to see an OAP that aggressive in pearls. Good luck.' He nods and jogs off towards his old banger of a car.

Flip and her brood continue their snaking dance around the front lawn and cheer when they see a huddle of friends walking down the path. 'Comrades!' Flip shouts, sprinting in their direction.

Lucy comes over with a bottle of water and a straw. 'Hydration for the human sacrifice. How are you bearing up?'

I blow my fringe out of my eyes. 'Not too bad. Counting down the minutes till the journalist gets here so I can say my piece and then get the feeling back in my fingers. But, you know, oddly proud.'

Luce squats down on the gravel and gives me an affectionate knee pat. 'You should be. You brought us all here in this lovely group. Weird, don't get me wrong, it's weird but I love it. This is our village, and we make arses of ourselves for it.' She flips one of her pigtails, tied up with bunting. 'I only wish Steve hadn't had to get into school early and miss it. Seeing you like this would have made his year.'

'Ha! He needs to absorb all the Connie-brand mess he can, because from this week onwards, I'm getting my shit together.'

Luce chewed the end of one of her bunches. 'I've always liked your shit exactly the way it is. But I'm glad you're going to get out there. Who knows where you might be, this time next year.'

'Maybe tied to a whole other gate.'

'Shut up. You could be working in a charity, maybe on a whole other continent.'

The itch was back and I tried wriggling on the spot to ease it. I mean, I could hardly look any more stupid, so what did I have to lose?

'Not so far away, I hope. I know it sounds a bit beauty queen, but when I went back up to Manchester it hit me that, OK, I'd ended up back in Hazlehurst because the magazine thing didn't work out and as a sort of favour to Gran – but that wasn't why I stayed. Not because I didn't have any better ideas, but because helping people is good for me. It feels good, in an almost selfish way.'

Luce rolls her eyes comically. 'And you just want world peace and to twirl your fiery batons?'

My publicity stunt pose means I'm helpless to whack her one for that.

She holds up her hands. 'Sorry, sorry. I ruined the moment. But I get it. And it's great, really, Cons. In an odd way, losing this place has been good for us. We found our bunting brotherhood, and it's kind of bounced you onto all sorts of other interesting things.'

I arch my neck to take a look back at the Hall. On a damp, gloomy morning it's not looking all that grand, a bit like a carefully folded swan napkin at the end of a boozy banquet meal: once a thing of beauty, now a bit sloppy and bashed up and all of a sudden useless.

It's time, Gran, I think. It's time to say goodbye, if we're honest. Let someone come in and build a brand new place, clean and shiny and pigeon-free. Or pour their money into fixing the plumbing and the subsidence and working out what on earth that sticky patch is at the back of the broom cupboard. We just didn't have that money, though we had the love.

And I might learn to love grabbing a super-hot venti seven minutes from our house.

'Choir's here!' Lucy bounces up. 'I'll go and help them off.'

I can hear a round robin of 'We shall not, we shall not be moved!' sung brightly if not tunefully from within the rusty minibus that's pulling up.

The gang are all here. We just need our press man to complete Bluebell Hall's final farewell. It might be goodbye, but it's a very loud one. I'm not reviewing gigs or planning festivals like I once dreamt, but I can plan an amazing event, alright. Maybe I'm not married just yet, but I don't think it's because I'm horribly deformed or broken inside: I just need to get out and go on some actual dates. That would help. The plan I've carved out for my future is a bit patchy, a bit hopeful, but I have the best friends in the world to help me get there. All in good time.

Chapter 21

Three months later

'If you're happy and you know it, make a noise!' The roar that hits me is a messy, lovely sound. Fifteen toddlers, a veritable hunting pack in less pleasant circumstances, are shaking tambourines and cowbells and maracas. The chubby babies on their mums' laps are doing their best to clap, though mostly just swiping air.

I move from a kneel to a cross-legged position, as I'd started to lose feeling in my legs in all the enjoyable hullabaloo. This new carpet is definitely a lot comfier than the old parquet. And one big bonus is that it's not my job to clean it at the end of the session. It turns out my goodbye to the Hall was pretty short-lived, all in all.

Marcus gave us a great write-up in the *Mirror* when we staged our sit in and the local *Shires Bugle* covered it too. After our MP retweeted a piece about the story, the coffee chain who'd just signed the papers on the Hall were so concerned about the bad PR, they gave Alex the go-ahead to offer us an olive branch: yes, the Hall would still become a mega coffee shop, but a part of the space would be given over twice a week to community projects! So we resurrected Sunday Fundays and the choir is still running too (all the elderly members still alive and kicking, I'm happy to say.) It was really a nifty thing to do, because the whole village instantly warmed to the change of ownership AND the company had a guaranteed stream of parental coffee addicts coming through their door. I haven't been able to persuade Susannah to try a mocha caramel latte with whipped cream just yet, though. She just sucks her lips in and mutters something about how tea is good enough for the Queen, so it's jolly well good enough for her.

I still have a weird urge to go into the broom cupboard and count the Brillo pads now and again, but seeing as it's now a ladies' loo cubicle, I can pull it off as needing to spend a cheeky penny. And I have to admit, it's lovely to see Bluebell Hall looking as fresh as a daisy. All the original features have been kept and gently restored, there's no whiff of damp, even on a wet day, and it has in its own way offered the community a place to be. The less edgy local teens are really glad to have a place to hang out that doesn't involve smoking in the woods or bullying children off the swings, and I've started to recognise some former Bluebells who now meet their mates here to have something trendy and skinny with a fat lot of gossip on the side. Flip has started a new sewing bee here one night a week and I make it to most of them, even though I still leave my thumb looking like Swiss cheese after any type of needlework. Polly is a dedicated member and is even learning how to adjust some of her mum's eighties stuff into one-offs that she can wear.

Things settled between Polly and Dom pretty swiftly after her return from Coventry. His blood-shot eyes and grey face at the door told her just how important she is to him, I think, and were a reminder that he didn't have everything locked away and forgotten about. Dom doesn't come along to the bee – he finally exhausted his tiny amount of enthusiasm for crafting when Flip suggested sewing phone cases out of tie-dyed denim – but he and Polly have a weekly ice skating date where they skate, talk and eat waffles. (The waffles come after.)

It's not something they ever did with Polly's mum, it's completely new to them, a memory that isn't tinged with sadness – but they also don't stop them-selves talking about the past as they whizz round on their blades with a background of lively pop. Dom told me he'd read a book about being a single parent dad and it advised that if you found talking about emotional stuff hard, try it when you were doing an activity that doesn't require constant eye contact. It's quite a nifty trick.

Polly has by no means magicked herself into a Swallows and Amazons teen – I've seen her huff and stomp away when someone else nabbed the last scrap of Liberty fabric at the sewing bee. But in my experience that is about as healthy as it gets for a fifteen-year-old, with the world and puberty to wrestle simultaneously.

–

After I left the Hall on that last day, with string burns around my wrists from where the bunting had begun to bite, I didn't go and interview with Annabel for the position of her nanny. Not that it wouldn't have been a rewarding thing to do in a different way, but it wasn't for me. It just felt... not quite enough. It would have felt wrong to make my world that limited. I wanted to be part of a bigger community, like I had through the Hall.

And I'm still trying to figure it out. I'm enrolled on a Charities Administration course that starts in October, in two months' time. If I want to get stuck in, I'm going to do it properly. I'll temp around my studies, so I can still help out with the household bills, and it might be a long road to a proper job in a proper organisation but I just feel in my bones that it's worth it. Caretaking on an epic scale. I want to organise events like the bunting bomb and the fete and even my human sacrifice stunt, to help raise cash and awareness for charities doing vital work. Kind of like masterminding festivals but with less glitter and more of a feel-good vibe the next day. But if I can find a way to work in live music and face-painting, all the better.

As the Sunday Funday troops file out the door, waving goodbye for another week, I let out a big sigh and stretch. 'Shutting up time, Jonnie?'

'At last.' The tattooed teen behind the barista's bar huffs, then adds, 'No offence.'

'None taken. I'm can't wait to clock off too. Having dinner round at my mates' house.'

He nods. 'Oh yeah. Happy birthday.'

He chucks a caramel waffle my way and I blush. 'You heartbreaker, Jon. See you same time, next week.'

With enrolling on my course and adjusting our finances, not to mention getting the community groups up and running in the 'new' Hall and settling the Bluebells in with the Scouts a little more permanently, I hadn't really thought about the big three oh approaching. So I was relieved when Steve said he'd cook me dinner at his place, just his family and me. That's basically my perfect bubble of fun right there, plus I'm dodging the pressure of organising some super amazing 30th bash that would probably see me in bed by 10.30 p.m. anyway. I want to organise events that put other people on a pedestal, not myself, thanks. It will be just Steve, Luce, Abel and me, homemade pizza and a game of Boggle. Delicious.

I've loved Stevie's homemade pizzas since he took A-Level Home Ec and produced the most amazing deep crust affair, covered in mozzarella and thick with anchovies. It might not be up everyone's street but it was up mine and right through the letterbox. Yum.

After I press their bell, I hear chairs being scraped back and Abel's squeaky protests. He must be trying his luck for a later bedtime. Maybe I could cash in some birthday favours on his behalf.

Then I hear Steve's trademark teacher exasperation shout, 'No!' just as a little hand pops through the letterbox. I crouch down to lock eyes with my favourite four-year-old.

'Can you just stay out here a bit. Your surprise isn't ready yet.'

'Abel!' Luce yells.

'But it isn't. We need to finish the bum tint.'

'Bunting?' I ask wearily. Honestly, I think I have seen enough of the stuff to last a lifetime. It's still taking up most of the love seat in the lounge at home. Mum's threatening to turn it into a big, cheery fishing net and put it in the car for her next trip to Devon.

'Ssshhhhh! It's a surprise,' Abel mouths the word.

'Well, she might as well come in, then!' Steve yanks opens the door and I'm hit with a wall of noise.

'Surprise!!!'

Here are all of my people, smiling at me. Not just Steve and his family, but Susannah, Flip and her husband, the WI crew, Polly hanging out with the A-level girls, Dom standing next to Alex. And even, right at the back, in the conservatory, jiggling on the spot and shaking her head apologetically, are Claire and a noisy Freddie.

Wow!

'Guys!' My voice wobbles as I step into the warm kitchen and take in the brilliant festivities: balloons in every corner with big, bold 30s printed all over them. A worktop full with bottles of booze huddled together, like commuters on a tube platform. Big bowls of my favourite Wotsits dotted within easy reach.

They start a bellowing rendition of 'Happy Birthday', with Abel's voice clearly audible in singing '– dear Ladyyyyyyy, happy birthday to you!' And finishing with a raspberry. Class.

The best bit, after seeing all my favourites, is the pizza. There's no bunting on the walls here, I'm glad to see, but the pizza is laid out, slice by slice jauntily angled, like glorious cheesy triangles of edible bunting. Quickly turning the paper tablecloth of the trestle table transparent with grease, so you know it's good. And between each pizza pennant are a few strings of linguini, as the bias binding! Genius.

I'm agog with wonder and greed. Luce leans in to whisper, 'I wouldn't actually eat the pasta, if I was you. Abel did that bit and he's been quite snotty this week.'

I jump on her with a fierce hug and she's almost knocked sideways.

'Oof! You're welcome, love. Couldn't let your big birthday pass without a little knees-up.'

Susannah pushes through the throng around the table with two glasses of something bubbly. 'Happy birthday, dear girl! Here's mud in your eye.'

We clink glasses and take big, thirsty gulps. 'Steady on, Susannah. Haven't you got work tomorrow?'

She bats my joke away with one well-manicured hand. 'Shush. You know fashion is run on booze, darling,' she says, enjoying drawing out the last word. 'Annabel has samples of her next Spring–Summer collection and she wants my opinion. So after a quick trip to the soft play, we'll put Alfred to bed and get onto the fine knits. I hardly call it work. It's such tremendous fun!' Her eyes twinkle as she knocks back another mouthful of fizz and I can see a glimpse of the 1970s Susannah. Not the shoulder pads as such, but the energy and the gumption.

I was feeling so bad about pulling out of the interview with Annabel at the last minute and only with the lame excuse of 'I've realised this is the last job in the world that I want.' So bad, in fact, I was about to call Susannah and ask for her help in how best to handle it with decorum. I was looking back and forth between her name on my phone and Annabel's ad, which mentioned her fashion business, when it hit me – Susannah was the perfect fit. She knew exactly what it was like to run a fashion empire AND master-mind a hectic family. She could support Annabel in both areas. Susannah would get a taste of the profession she missed and Annabel would get a seasoned pro as a nanny who was unlikely to want to steal her husband from under her roof. Win win.

It all seems to be going swimmingly so far (Susannah credits being partially deaf in one ear with how she rubs along with Alfred so well) and Annabel was so delighted with how things turned out, she's even promised me a free kaftan. Is that a good thing? I'm still not sure.

'Presents!' Abel squeals. 'Cake! Presents! Lady!'

Stevie pats the top of Abel's head with a firm hand, to try and keep his son within the same ten-foot vicinity. 'Remember, it's not for you, Abie. And it might not be what you consider a present.'

I have a slice of pizza halfway to my eager gob. 'Presents! Cake! Bring it all to me! I'm the birthday lady, after all.'

'Your wish is our command!' Steve booms. 'Where are the present bearers?' Polly and her mates give matching sighs of distaste. A primary school teacher has no pull on them. Polly passes a big, squashy package up over the table, to me. 'It's like… You know. For you, and junk.'

Susannah moves some of the pizza away gingerly, so I have room to unwrap. Inside the multi-coloured paper is the most beautiful quilt I'd ever seen.

'Oh. It's for your bed,' Abel says, his voice low and sad. 'I wanted you to get *Paws Patrol*.' His hair gets rigorously tussled until he runs away.

The quilt is made up of light blue squares, each one with a different handwritten message that someone has stitched over. I can see the simple scrawl of some of my Bluebells, Veronica's unbelievably neat hand, happy birthday messages from all of the Society members and 'Congrats on getting old! ;)' from Polly. My eyes are too blurred from tears to read them all properly.

The deep border is a zigzag affair and I realise it's made of sewn-up bunting triangles. A dent in my stash I hadn't even clocked. Crafty!

I run my hand over the bunting bits, the stitching, the fabric suffused with care and love. 'Oh. Oh… It's. The. Best!'

'Just to stop you crying, here's the cake,' Steve quickly interjects, passing me a round chocolate sponge. 'Don't weep into the icing. It's a very nice ganache.'

'Caaaaaaaaake!' shouts Abel and the party has begun.

The pizza slipped down in the way only delicious, greasy food really can. The cake didn't last much longer. I was three glasses of fizz and a rum and Coke down when I finally worked my way round to Alex in the conservatory. He had been given Freddie jiggling duties, as Claire was hoovering up the last cake crumbs and gabbing to Steve about all my embarrassing birthday fails of the past. Oh joy. It almost dented my amazing happiness at seeing her again. Almost, but not quite. I had missed this brilliant woman in my life, so much. At least my little bonkers trip up to Manchester had made me realise that and reminded me to keep in touch more regularly. We now have an 'Ork' WhatsApp group, for her to send me daily Freddie updates.

'It's in the knees,' I whisper to Alex. Freddie is leaving the most adorable dribble marks on his polo shirt.

'I'm learning that. I'm knackered,' he whispers back. 'Joe Wicks should put this in his HIIT routine. Baby bouncing then half an avocado. Happy birthday, by the way.'

'Thanks. This is great.'

He bounces lightly from foot to foot, Freddie held softly but safely against him. Stirring memories of Athena posters are coming to mind. 'And were you genuinely surprised?'

'Oh yes. I mean, who could guess they'd have pizza bunting, but no *Paws Patrol*?'

'I've got something for you. In my pocket.'

'Um, what?! I haven't heard that line since 2007. And even then it wasn't new.'

His cheeks colour. 'Actually in my pocket. An actual present. But I can't reach it right now.' He nods towards the little fleshy bundle.

'Ah. Shall I?' I gingerly reach my hand into Alex's back pocket, suddenly feeling the eyes of everyone in the room on me.

It's a slim little present, definitely too hard to be made of bunting. I peel back the brown paper wrapping to see a lanyard.

'OK. Thank you?'

Alex winces as Freddie twitches in his sleep. In a tiny croak he says, 'An internship, at the Hibbert Foundation. You'll need that to get into the office. If you want it, that is. I know you want to build up your charity experience, so I thought you could see how the money is allocated and spent. It's not UNICEF exactly, but it's a start.'

All I can do is blink for a few moments. 'Wow, yes. Please, and thank you! That is so... amazing. Thank you.'

'You said that.'

'Well I mean it double.'

Alex continues to sway back and forth on his heels, a human rocking horse. 'And don't worry about me cramping your style, I'm off in a few weeks. Seconded to another hospice charity.'

'Oh.' I turn the clear plastic badge over and over in my hands. 'The Scouts will be gutted.'

He smiles sheepishly. 'Well, I'm not going as in 'going from Hazlehurst'. I'm going to commute into London. Pretty much feel at home now, what with my encyclopaedic knowledge of the Flames N Chips menu. Plus, the boys never got round to covering Caitlin Moran in their skit, so I can't just leave them hanging.'

'I was going to say. It would irresponsible not to teach them a bit of modern feminism, alongside the woggle tying.'

Alex swallows his laugh. 'Do you actually know what a woggle is?'

'Nope. And do not tell me. I might be 30 but I'm not ready for that. Have you got a drink, by the way? Claire used the whole 'ugh my arms ache' sympathy trick, I take it?'

He shakes his head. 'Nothing as subtle as that. She just straight up said 'hold this and keep moving' and went. So here I am. Don't suppose you want to switch?' He mugged an exhausted grimace.

'Ahhh. No. It's my birthday! I have to drink and be merry, and that just doesn't mix with tiny babies and their soft skulls. Sorry.' At the mention of soft skulls, he goes a bit pale. 'But I will get you a drink. Hang on.'

Over at the kitchen counter I'm pouring Alex a beer from the local brewery, Horny Goat's Revenge. Claire and Stevie pincer me.

'What did that bloke give you?' Claire pokes me unnecessarily hard in the arm.

'Ow! Nosey.'

I fill her in and she fiddles with a strand of shiny, clean hair. Sleep and showers must be in greater supply these days as Freddie nears six months. 'A thoughtful present. That's interesting, right, Steve? He put real care and effort into it.'

'Hmm. Real care and effort. And he comes out to the pub with us now, you know. Connie invites him.' Steve nods smugly.

'Does she now? Well, hello hello.'

The beer ends up with a stupidly thick head, like my two best friends here. 'Tweedledee and Tweedle-dummy, get to the point.'

Steve splutters. 'That's rich! You two have been dancing around each other for months, laughing about your Scout Hut antics, buying each other roasted peanuts in the Handsome Hog.' He grabs me by the shoulders and shakes me with each word. 'Ask. Him. Out. Luce and I are out of box sets and we need a new plot line to become obsessed with. Your romance will do.'

Before I can work out my rebuttal, Claire leaps in. 'And not just to the pub or some greasy place for chips. A date where you have to change your clothes and redo your deodorant. Maybe go to his place for dinner and a movie?'

Steve points at her, adding, 'I believe they now call that Netflix and chill.'

I grab the glass of beer; it's developing a sweat to match my top lip. I mumble something about ridicu-lous local busybodies and barge my way back to Alex.

'Horny Goat's Revenge.'

Alex manoeuvres Freddie a bit higher up onto his shoulder, still dead asleep with an open, wet gob, so he can thirstily gulp back half the pint. 'Thank god. And, you know, I think they're right.'

'Huh?'

'Your friends. This place is full but the acoustics are pretty good. We should go out, right?'

I can feel my skin flushing around my ears and jaws. What would Taylor Swift do? I think.

'Um. We should. Am I asking you or are you asking me?'

He bites his bottom lip for a moment. 'Does it matter?'

'Nope.'

'Exactly. So, Friday, then? The Giggling Squid in Marlow is a pretty good Thai, my boss tells me. And you most certainly need to wear deodorant to go there. I can come and pick you up in my Fiesta. After that and a few spring rolls, I reckon you'll be swooning all over the shop.'

I can't help but laugh. 'Wow. A softer side to the Scout Master. Who would have known.'

Alex changes up his swaying pattern to side to side. 'I'm nice. When have I ever not been nice?'

'Um, the day of the Easter parade? You blanked me. It was totally public and embarrassing. And you were all mardy at the May Day fete with Flip and me. Told us we were unprofessional. Not that nice, all in all. I don't feel so bad now for calling you the Demon Scout Master behind your back.'

He studies the grey star pattern on Freddie's sleep suit with unnecessary scrutiny. 'Ah, well the parade thing is simple to explain, actually. I knew I was about to deliver some pretty bad news to you and I thought I should retain some professional distance, for the public image of the Scouts, at least.'

'I get that. I suppose. But the mood change at the fete? You'd been quite pleasant, for you, up until that point.'

He winces a little and some pretty cute lines gather at the corner of his eyes. 'I was a bit jealous of that journalist guy. And it sounded like you were going to ask him out…'

I clamp both hands over my mouth so my bark of laughter can't wake Freddie but the noise gets lost anyway in a cheer as the front door opens. 'Where's my birthday girl?' I hear my mum ask. Over my shoulder I see her barging through the crowd, her Devon tan adding an extra twinkle to her eyes. Sheila's brother got back on his feet ages ago, but Mum has made fortnightly trips down there, shifts permitting. It doesn't take Jessica Fletcher to know what's going on beside the seaside.

'Not now!' I hear Steve hiss. 'She's actually sorting out her love life for once!'

Mum freezes in her tracks and starts to edge backwards, mouthing 'Sorry! Sorry!' Susannah hands her a glass of fizz and pulls her into a little group to talk tan lines.

Alex exhales over the top of Freddie's head, sending a little Mexican Wave through his fuzzy hair. 'Well, that's a relief.'

'What is?'

'Well, at least our date can't be the most awkward moment of my life now.'

–

Hours later, with the food scoffed and the drinks drunk, it's just Luce and me on the sofa, Steve washing up and occasionally chipping into our conversation from his rightful place at the sink. Everyone else has gone home and I've recounted my date plans with Alex for the third time. I've so far denied her suggestion of putting the whole evening on Facebook Live.

I managed to grab some time with my mum while the party was still loud and busy. Her time beside the seaside was really paying off – her skin was biscuity brown, her eyes were clear and bright and she'd started wearing all manner of nautical-themed jumpers, which I could let slide because she was so happy. But before I could compliment her on all this, she took me by the shoulders, held me at arm's length and said, 'You look so peachy, my girl. It's because you found your sunshine.' And with a wink, she headed back towards another white wine spritzer and a gossip with Susannah. It was the cherry on top of my birthday cake to see her so full of vim and vigour.

Though I don't think I could fit in another slice of actual cake right now. I'm in the sugar-coma stage of post-party bliss. Lucy and I have got my amazing birthday quilt over our knees and Abel is snoring on his bed upstairs, a Paws Patrol figure tucked under his chin awkwardly. Love that kid.

Luce's eyelids are fluttering closed, but she's fighting it. 'Wow. That was a day.' She smiles.

I stretch my arms above my head. 'I know. Pizza, cake, presents. Even some work experience.'

'A date.' She points at me, like I might forget.

'That too. And you know, when I spoke to my mum, she pretty much let slip she and Peter are a proper item. Do you date in your fifties? Or do you just move straight into shared jigsaws and slippers?'

'Let me know,' Steve hollers, 'because I might need to get ahead of this for my second wife.'

'Ho ho ho! With dad jokes this good you'd think you had twenty children, instead of just the one.'

'Two!' Steve shouts back.

'One and a quarter,' Lucy corrects him as my face pulls into a series of confused scrunches. 'I'm pregnant! Boy, that was a weird way to tell you. But I didn't want to overshadow your birthday.'

'Are you kidding?! This is brilliant! Oh wait—' I tuck the blanket fully around her and move a footstool under her ankles. 'How do you feel? What do you need?'

'Oh no no no!' She wags a finger at me. 'No caretaking tonight. In fact, no amateur caretaking full stop. You're starting a whole new decade and a whole new career,'

Steve singsongs over his suds, '– and maybe a whole new rooooooomance!'

'Yes, and that. You're no longer responsible for everyone else in your life being happy and sorted, just yourself. Capiche?'

Steve comes in and takes a seat on the armrest of the saggy sofa. 'I love it when she talks like a pint-sized mobster. But she has a point. You've done your bit for Hazlehurst, Cons. Now it's time to be the caretaker of Connie Duncan and only Connie Duncan.'

I look at the knackered but contented faces of two of my best friends. And I think of Flip tucking her noisy brood into bed, and Susannah casting her eye over cigarette pants and camel coats. Polly stitching words of love by day and skating with Dom by night. The bouncing babies at the coffee shop (and – squee! – having Lucy and the new baby join them soon). Mum digging her toes in the sand, side by side with a tall, balding man. And yes, even the briefest image of Alex and a bowl of prawn crackers comes to mind.

This is my community. This is my Hazlehurst. I'm so lucky to be here.

And don't worry, Gran, even if they tell me to stop taking care of them, I'm still going to do it. Just a bit. When they're not looking.

Acknowledgements

Thank you to my amazingly supportive and inspiringly productive writerly mates – Juliet Ashton, Michele Gorman, Victoria Fox, Kirsty Greenwood and Vanessa Greene being those with the most saintly patience required to be able to listen to me over the years.

Thank you to my parents and partner for giving me lots of coffee shop breaks from Mum Duty so I could disappear into Hazlehurst and put Connie through her paces. Thank you to the lovely Pret team near my office who didn't mind me stretching out one cup of tea every morning while I beavered away on my trusty laptop! See you again soon…

A huge and heartfelt thank you to Louise Cullen at Canelo, an editor with the gentlest but wisest approach, for taking a chance on this book. I hope it repays your trust and then some. It's a privilege to be published, and I'm still pinching myself. Also big thanks to Iain Millar, Michael Bhaskar, Nick Barreto and Simon Collinson for all your amazing work and for welcoming me into the Canelo family. I feel very lucky to be here. And not forgetting massive massive thanks to Sarah for opening the door to Canelo for me.

And thank you to YOU, lovely reader, for buying this book. I hope it brings a bit of fun to your commute or tea break or bath. And if leaves you with an urge to make bunting – even better!